She looked beautiful. That much hadn't changed.

But it was the *only* thing that hadn't changed.

"How's Toby doing?" she asked as she popped the top on a can of Rowdy's favorite soda.

"Sleeping again. He's really cute. Still sucking his fist, even when he's napping."

Angelica handed Rowdy the soda and took Toby into her arms, landing a soft kiss on her baby's cheek before gently placing him in his car seat so she and Rowdy would have their hands free to eat.

"Still your favorite?" she asked, gesturing toward his soda can.

He lifted the can in salute. "I'm surprised you remembered."

Another flash of pain crossed her gaze. "I remember a lot, if truth be told."

So did he.

And he really, *really* wished he didn't. Because with every unexpected glimpse into their past, every unanticipated memory, it became harder and harder to catch a breath.

He hadn't been ready to see her again.

And he wasn't sure he ever would be.

A *Publishers Weekly* bestselling and award-winning author with over 1.5 million books in print, **Deb Kastner** writes stories of faith, family and community in a small-town Western setting. She lives in Colorado with her husband and a pack of miscreant mutts, and is blessed with three daughters and two grandchildren. She enjoys spoiling her grandkids, movies, music (The Texas Tenors!), singing in the church choir and exploring Colorado on horseback.

Books by Deb Kastner

Love Inspired

Cowboy Country

Yuletide Baby
The Cowboy's Forever Family
The Cowboy's Surprise Baby
The Cowboy's Twins
Mistletoe Daddy
The Cowboy's Baby Blessing
And Cowboy Makes Three

Christmas Twins

Texas Christmas Twins

Email Order Brides

Phoebe's Groom
The Doctor's Secret Son
The Nanny's Twin Blessings
Meeting Mr. Right

Visit the Author Profile page at Harlequin.com for more titles.

And Cowboy Makes Three

Deb Kastner

HARLEQUIN® LOVE INSPIRED®

Recycling programs
for this product may
not exist in your area.

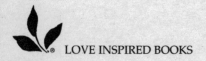

LOVE INSPIRED BOOKS

ISBN-13: 978-1-335-50953-6

And Cowboy Makes Three

www.Harlequin.com

Printed in U.S.A.

But I trusted in thee, O Lord:
I said, Thou art my God.
My times are in thy hand.
—*Psalms* 31:14–15

To my dear friend Lisa Palmer.
We've kept each other sane through the years
and I am blessed to call you my friend.
You are one of the strongest people I know.
Keep fighting the good fight!

Chapter One

⟨❧⟩

Angelica May Carmichael had been duped.

By her own grandmother.

She looked around and sighed in exasperation. This wasn't a picnic.

Or rather, this wasn't *just* a picnic, though there were brightly colored baskets covered in ribbons dotting the lawn all across the community green.

Not a picnic. *Picnics.*

And this wasn't a quiet, personal outing with Granny's best friend, Jo Spencer, as Angelica had been given to expect, either. Not that an outing with the boisterous old redhead who owned Cup O' Jo's Café could ever be labeled as *quiet*. That woman wouldn't know quiet if it bit her on the nose.

But a private picnic?

Yeah, not so much.

In hindsight, Angelica realized she should have gone with her gut feeling and headed straight to Granny's ranch instead of stopping in at Cup O' Jo's to let Jo know she'd arrived safely. A phone call would have sufficed.

But no. Jo had been adamant she come straight to the café, sounding a bit *too* enthusiastic about seeing her again. Everything about Jo Spencer was enthusiastic, but her suggestion had been overanimated even for Jo.

She'd even anticipated Angelica's hesitation, telling her to slip through the back door of the café. She'd assured her that she wouldn't be seen by any customers, and that her nephew, Chance, the cook who would no doubt be in the kitchen, would keep their secret. He wasn't much of talker, anyway.

If only she hadn't been in such a hurry to get into town and out again without being seen that she hadn't recognized the signals, the internal alarms blaring in her head.

Their meeting was only supposed to be her and Jo. Having been Granny's best friend, Jo understood Angelica's dilemma at returning to Serendipity at all—or at least Angelica had thought she had.

"Oh, honey, welcome back," Jo had said, hugging her so hard it pressed the breath right out of her lungs. "And let me see sweet Toby."

Jo had exclaimed over the newborn and then had handed her a letter written by her recently deceased granny, addressed with only Angelica's first name and scribbled in Granny's chicken-scratch handwriting.

"Consider it a last request," Jo had suggested.

Directions?

More like a cryptic note.

Picnic With Jo.

It was a strange thing to ask, but Angelica figured it was the least she could do since she hadn't been able to be there for Granny's last days—or even her funeral.

If she hadn't followed the instructions out of love for Granny, she would have followed them out of guilt.

Which was why she had found herself smack-dab in the middle of a full-fledged town event, Toby tucked into a front pack.

Serendipity did their parties up right, and, as usual, nearly everyone in town was present, enjoying every moment of the event. Here in Serendipity, a person could expect to find a lot of love and laughter.

But even as a youth, Angelica had struggled to capture the happy spirit of the town celebrations. And no wonder. For as long as she could remember, she'd been the town pariah, as well as her family's.

And after the catastrophic series of events that sent her fleeing Serendipity on the eve of her own wedding rehearsal, well, she didn't expect *anyone* to forgive her—least of all her ex-fiancé, sheep farmer Rowdy Masterson.

Standing right in the middle of a large crowd of people, most of whom had known her back in the day and had no doubt *not* forgotten her or her mistakes, was exactly the type of situation Angelica had most wished to avoid.

Thankfully, the event in progress was an auction, with Jo as auctioneer. Something about making money for a new senior center. Everyone was busy watching the platform, where one of the young bachelors on the docket was flexing his biceps for a very appreciative crowd.

Just as long as it kept *her* out of the limelight, she was good. She'd come back home to Serendipity on the sly, for one weekend only, with a deliberate and strategic agenda. Since she would be staying at Granny's now abandoned sheep farm, she hadn't expected to see anyone other than Jo Spencer, who had been named the executor of Granny's estate, and Granny's lawyer, Matthew MacPherson, who would guide her in whatever next steps she needed to take to fulfill the terms of Granny's will—and to sell the ranch.

She'd most definitely had no intention of interacting with all the people who'd known her *back then*. People who would stand as judge and jury on the way she'd lived her life—especially since she'd arrived back in town with a baby in tow and no ring on her finger.

She didn't understand what was going on right now. She and Granny had planned to get together this precise weekend, even before Granny's health had taken such a downhill spiral. She had the sinking feeling Granny had something planned for this auction, something that Jo was now tasked with making sure Angelica followed through on.

Angelica might not be able to avoid the crowd today, but she prayed with her whole heart that she'd at least be able to steer clear of Rowdy. She didn't want to be responsible for suddenly triggering thoughts in Rowdy of a painful past he would no doubt rather forget.

She didn't want to hurt him. Not for the world.

Because long ago, in her youth, she had been in love with him, believing they were soul mates who would grow old together, live happily-ever-after.

Until she'd ruined everything.

Anyway, he'd probably moved on with his life. Perhaps he had even married and started a family. She'd been too ashamed to ask Jo how Rowdy was doing. She was grateful that, so far, she hadn't laid eyes on him, and she hoped to keep it that way.

Her stomach churned like a combine across her nerves and it was all she could do not to be sick. Not for the first time that day, she wondered if she ought not leave before someone recognized her.

Her soft pink hoodie was made of a light cotton material, but she felt uncomfortably warm and stifled as she stood near the back of the crowd on the small-town community green, attempting to remain incognito while surreptitiously watching to make sure Rowdy was nowhere in the vicinity.

Up to this point, no one had appeared to take much notice of her, as everyone's attention was still completely absorbed in what was taking place upon the wooden platform currently serving as an improvised auction site.

Serendipity, Texas's First Annual Bachelors and Baskets Auction was already well under way, with many bachelors—and several married men, as well—already lassoed off the stage and into the care of their winning bidders, ladies beaming and cheering in delight over their triumphant purchases.

What had started as a regular bachelor auction had quickly expanded to include married men offering their skills at fixing dilapidated houses or old cars. The ladies could bid on whatever man had the skills to match their projects.

Several of the cuter bachelors had been purchased not so much for their practical skills as their good looks and the possibility of a date. The single ladies weren't about to pass up such a grand opportunity.

Not to be outdone by the men, the local women had offered to share decorated picnic baskets brimming with good, homemade country cooking with the fellows they won.

Which explained the picnic.

She wished Granny was still around to explain to her what all this was about. Why had Granny wanted her here?

But then, if Granny was still around, Angelica wouldn't be conspicuously standing in the middle of the community green, feeling as if she had a fluorescent sign flashing over her head announcing her return.

Prodigal Daughter's Homecoming.

Out of nowhere, guilt assaulted Angelica, burning her insides. Through no fault of her own, she'd had to miss the end of Granny's life and even her funeral. But that didn't stop her from feeling bad about it.

Regretful.

Too little, too late.

If only Granny had lived long enough to see this weekend with Angelica. How different life would be then.

She held on to her new faith by the tips of her fingers, but there was so much she still didn't understand. God's ways were different than man's, but how could He have let this happen, just when she'd discovered the joy of knowing Christ?

Granny was still supposed to be alive. When she'd suddenly fallen gravely ill, Angelica had wanted to rush to her side, but there had been complications with the pregnancy and she couldn't travel.

Granny had insisted everything would be okay.

But it *hadn't* been okay.

Granny had passed far too soon.

Oh, how she would have loved her namesake, precious Toby Francis Carmichael. Angelica's heart broke every time she thought about it.

They'd intended this weekend to be a special get-together so Granny could meet Toby, but she'd passed away the very day Toby was born.

Since Angelica's travel plans had already been made, she hadn't seen any reason to change or cancel them. She had come home to pay her respects and meet with the lawyer, not attend a party.

Get in and get out. And the less people who knew about it—about *her*—the better.

The whole atmosphere was charged with joy and excitement, but Angelica, with a baseball cap pulled low over her brow and her hoodie over that, wasn't feeling either one of those emotions.

It had been eight long, painful years since the last time she'd attended a Serendipity function.

Her heart clenched and her emotions took a nosedive. She'd never been anything more to this town than the token troublemaker, no matter how hard she'd tried to change people's opinions of her.

Eventually she'd stopped trying.

Despite Angelica's faults—and what she now realized was a defensively bad attitude—Granny had understood her.

And Rowdy had loved her.

Had being the operative word.

Her thoughts were abruptly called back to the present when Toby, tucked reassuringly close to her shoulder, sighed in his sleep and sucked on his fist, momentarily shifting Angelica's attention away from the platform. Toby was such a sweet, beautiful baby, a real blessing in every possible regard.

Granted, as his mother, Angelica knew she was a little bit biased.

"If I can have your attention, please," Jo announced, pounding a gavel against a podium that had been brought over from the town hall. "We still have several fellows lookin' to be bid on here and a senior center still needin' to be built. And who knows? The best guys might be yet to come. You don't want to miss out on your perfect match 'cause you're too busy jawin' with your neighbors."

Since Jo was serving as the auctioneer, she had ditched Angelica with not so much as a second glance, much less an explanation.

It shouldn't bother her to be left alone. She'd been on her own most of her adult life. But it hurt her nonetheless. Maybe because she felt she was underneath an unseen spotlight.

Or maybe because Jo was a friend.

Angelica had been left to the mercy of the throng as it grew tighter toward the platform, pushing her with them. Her anxiety level rose exponentially as she became farther engulfed by the crowd.

So much for a calm, peaceful picnic.

Angelica pulled Toby a little closer, murmuring soft nonsense words in his ear and tucking her head close to his, inhaling his sweet, soothing baby scent. She reassured herself with the thought that, very soon, this would all be over and she could hightail it out of town and back to Denver where she belonged.

Or not *belonged*, really. She didn't fit in anywhere. But at least she wasn't under the constant judgment she felt sure she would find here in Serendipity.

"All right, folks," Jo announced with a boisterous

bounce in her step that sent her red curls bobbing. When the crowd didn't immediately quiet, she pounded her gavel on the podium several times until she was certain she had everyone's attention.

"Next up on the docket," she called, her voice over-riding the little section of the crowd that was still speaking, "is a Serendipity fan favorite, especially among the ladies. Drumroll, please. Let's hear it for Rowdy Masterson!"

Angelica's breath froze in her lungs as she slowly raised her head.

Rowdy.

At the first sight of him, her heart jolted to life and then dropped like a boulder to the pit of her stomach, where it rumbled around disturbingly.

The crowd roared as Rowdy stepped up onto the makeshift wooden platform, his mouth creased in a friendly grin. Much had changed over the years, but not Rowdy's smile.

A shiver of awareness vibrated through Angelica at her first glimpse of the man she knew so well, and paradoxically, didn't know at all.

Rowdy.

Angelica cringed as he stepped forward, still slightly favoring his left leg when he walked.

So his injury had never completely healed, then. The inside of her head reverberated, her guilt clanging like a gong, and a wave of nausea washed through her.

Rowdy's injury?

That was all on her.

It was enough to shatter her heart all over again.

Yet another prayer left unanswered. She had so wanted Rowdy to be healed completely of his injuries.

If it hadn't been for her pressing him to participate in the saddle bronc event he hadn't been prepared for, he wouldn't be limping in the first place.

Other than the way he clearly put additional effort into moving his left leg over his right, time had been good to him. He was as handsome as ever, with thick wavy blond hair and warm blue eyes. Strong planes defined his masculine face, weathered from the sun and shaded with a couple days' growth of beard, giving him a rugged air.

He'd filled out in the years since she'd last seen him. His shoulders were broader and his muscles more defined from ranch work.

Not surprisingly, Rowdy didn't have to entertain the crowd by doing tricks or flexing his muscles to get their attention, as other men before him had done. He merely flashed them his signature toothy grin and gestured with his fingers for his rapt audience to increase their applause. The resulting hoots, catcalls and laughter made Rowdy's grin widen epically, and he tipped his hat in appreciation.

She remembered Rowdy's smile all too well, along with the whispered words of a happy future meant just for the two of them alone to share.

An ugly, dark feeling churned in her gut and she swallowed hard against the bile that burned in her throat.

She counted those days as nothing more than the naïveté of youth, when they still thought they had their whole lives before them and that they could weather any storm life threw at them as long as they were together.

When they'd believed they were invincible.

They hadn't yet comprehended that life could change in a moment.

But they'd learned. Oh, how painfully they'd learned.

It had only taken one second for their whole world to come crashing down around them.

One second.

And some things a person never recovered from—physically, emotionally or spiritually.

"Hush down, now," Jo called, rapping her gavel to regain control of the crowd. "Quiet!"

A group of laughing young women near the front of the crowd immediately started bidding on Rowdy, cheerfully one-upping each other before Jo could officially open the bidding.

"Wait, wait. No bids, please," Jo said, holding her hands up to stop the ladies from continuing.

The noise of the crowd immediately dropped to a hushed whisper.

"We've got a special case here with Rowdy, today," Jo continued. "I'm sorry to disappoint all you single ladies out there, but Rowdy has already been bought and paid for before this auction even began."

People gasped in astonishment.

"That's not fair," came a youngish-sounding female voice from the crowd. "No one else got to do that with any of the other men."

The crowd rumbled in agreement.

Angelica continued to keep her head low but her ears were perfectly attuned to Jo's words. She had a lot of questions that she was certain were echoing through the crowd.

Who had enough wherewithal to convince Jo to bend the rules of the auction?

Maybe a better question would be—*how?*

Jo tended to rule with an iron fist when she was in charge of an event—which she usually was. Between the two of them, Jo and her husband, Frank, the head of the town council, kept Serendipity running smoothly.

The old redhead was as stubborn as the day was long, and most people in town wouldn't even conceive of trying to change her mind once she'd gone and decided what was what. There was no arguing with her. And she was a stickler for rules—at least when it suited her.

Apparently today it suited her to make up her own new set of rules.

Jo snorted and shook her head, laughing at the negative reaction of the townspeople. She didn't even try to explain herself.

Not good old Jo Spencer.

Instead, she gestured for Rowdy to remove his hat, hitched up the rope in her palm—the one waiting for the winning bidder to lasso their catch with—and expertly flicked the noose around Rowdy, tugging the line tight around his shoulders.

Angelica was impressed with Jo's roping skills. The old woman ran a café, not a ranch. Clearly, she'd been practicing, and apparently, Angelica guessed, whatever was happening here with Rowdy was the reason. She'd known beforehand that she would have to trick rope this particular pony.

Without so much as looking back to see if he was following, she snapped the line taut and led him off the platform, the crowd parting before her.

He was being ushered off to who knows where like a lamb to the slaughter, Angelica thought.

Rowdy didn't resist. Why would he?

He had to be at least as curious as the murmuring crowd as to the identity of the woman who'd purchased him. *Someone* had cared an awful lot to go to the trouble, not to mention expense, of buying Rowdy in such an unconventional fashion.

Angelica didn't even want to know. And she absolutely ignored the sting of envy that whipped through her.

She had no right.

Rowdy was in her past, something she would rather not revisit right now.

Or ever.

She had enough on her plate just caring for Toby—and now trying to figure out how best to put the Carmichael property to market and still honor Granny's last wishes.

She appreciated the money she'd been left along with the land, and she knew Granny had been thinking of Toby when she'd written that part of her will. But Toby was special and would never run a sheep farm—and Angelica certainly couldn't. She was the furthest thing from a rancher as it was possible for her to be.

She was a pastor's kid—and not a very good one—who had grown up to be simple hotel banquet server. Not the best job ever, but it paid the bills. And as a single mother, she couldn't afford to be picky.

The obvious solution was to sell the ranch that had been in the family for generations, and then pocket the money to use on Toby's future—a future that didn't include working with sheep.

Gramps had died young of a heart attack and Granny's only son, Angelica's father, Richard, had chosen the pastorate over sheep farming, leaving Granny Frances to work the land well past the time she ought to have retired.

Angelica would have been able to save the day merely by marrying Rowdy as she'd once intended to do. They'd planned to join their land together, since his family were sheepherders, as well.

But she hadn't.

And they didn't.

Instead, she'd run away and in the process dashed the hopes and dreams of more than one person.

That for even one moment she'd considered being a rancher's wife without the slightest idea of what that meant, how to work with the sheep and tend to the land, was just one of many ways she'd showcased her youthful ignorance.

It had been all about love, as defined by a woman too young to know how to recognize it.

Pie in the sky, a twinkle in her eye and zero common sense.

Whatever love was, that couldn't have been it.

Rowdy probably thanked the Lord every day that she hadn't saddled him with her utter incompetence as a rancher and a life partner, not to mention her bad reputation across town.

No. As bad as it had been, and still was, she had done him a favor, even if he now hated her for it.

She'd cut those ties. Then her parents had virtually disowned her. Granny was all she had left after she'd left town, and for many years, she'd been too ashamed even to reach out to her.

After she'd discovered she was pregnant with Toby, she had made her life right with Christ and she had reached out for Granny, who had welcomed her back with open arms and a loving and forgiving heart. But Angelica had never gotten back home to see her.

Not in time. Granny had passed away when Toby was born. She hadn't known that Toby would have special needs, be preciously different, and that God meant him for other things.

Extraordinary things.

But not sheep farming.

That was one prayer that would never be answered. Not as Granny had wanted it to be, anyway.

Angelica sighed. No matter how she looked at it, nor how much grief she felt at letting Granny Frances down, selling the ranch was the only conceivable answer to her dilemma—the only one that worked in the best interests of both Angelica and Toby. She was sorry not to be able to fulfill Granny's wishes, but that was just how it had to be.

She had to think of Toby first.

She still had no idea why Jo had brought her here to the auction, when she should be at Granny's ranch putting her affairs in order.

As far as she was concerned, it was well past the time for her to leave the community green and the auction behind and return to Granny's ranch house, where she could mull over her problems in private, release the thunder of emotions that had been hovering over her like a huge black storm cloud all morning.

With her decision made, she turned away from the platform and started walking back toward the street where she'd parked her sedan, knowing Frank would give Jo a ride home.

At the moment, the effervescent old redhead had her

hands full with the auction—and, more specifically, with a rope full of Rowdy.

"Angelica May. Wait!"

Angelica skidded to a halt at Jo's use of her middle name. The only other person in the world who had called her Angelica May had been Granny, God rest her soul.

Tears sprang unbidden into Angelica's eyes at the many happy memories that instantly flashed through her mind. Granny loved Serendipity get-togethers and would have been bidding up a storm on behalf of the senior center—probably snatching up one of the good-looking young bachelors from right under the nose of a pretty, single woman.

And then, knowing Granny, she'd have him mucking stalls for her just so she could admire his muscular physique. Gramps had always been the only man for Granny and she'd never married again, but that hadn't meant she couldn't enjoy what the good Lord put in front of her eyes. She was old, not blind, she used to say, and then she and Jo Spencer would cackle over their shared joke.

With the well of deep emotion fractured, grief rolled into anger and Angelica stiffened. The scene unfolding in front of her became increasingly obvious with every step Jo took. She was dragging Rowdy right to Angelica's side.

Angelica didn't dash away, even if every nerve in her body was urging her to do so. Question after question pressed her down.

Why was this happening? Jo had to know there was no possible way any variation of this scenario would turn out well.

Angelica mumbled unintelligible words under her breath, quietly venting her frustration with the situation, but her throat closed around her air and it came out sounding like she was choking on carbonated soda.

So much for remaining incognito.

Now the whole town would know she was here. And she knew she wouldn't be welcomed back with open arms.

Especially not after what she'd done to Rowdy.

Even as a teenager, Rowdy had been popular in town. And from what she'd seen today, with everyone cheering and all those young ladies bidding for some time with him, that hadn't changed.

Rowdy was one of Serendipity's favorite sons.

Angelica...*wasn't.*

She hadn't been well liked, nor had she been understood. No one in town other than Granny, Jo and Rowdy had ever given her a fair shot.

Now everyone would think she'd captured Rowdy at auction in some underhanded fashion that was unfair to the rest of the crowd.

And the fact that she'd shown up in town unmarried and with a baby?

This was *so* not going to work out well for her.

Oh, why had she ever come home to Serendipity at all?

She turned in time to see Rowdy digging in his heels, his cowboy boots raising dust. His brow was deeply furrowed and his lips were set in a hard line.

Yep. Not happy to see her.

Surprise, surprise.

Jo, however, wasn't taking Rowdy's reluctance as an answer. The more he balked like a mule, the harder she pulled. She stopped in front of a gaping Angelica and dropped the rope into her hand, pressing a sealed envelope into her palm at the same time.

"This particular letter is addressed to the both of you," Jo informed them, pointing to Granny's unmistakable script on the front of the envelope.

Angelica and Rowdy.

Angelica folded it in two and shoved it into the back pocket of her jeans without another look. Her mind was turning so fast she was getting dizzy. She couldn't get her head around what all this meant.

Buying Rowdy at auction before the auction even started. Leaving a note for the two of them.

What part did Granny have in all this? Was she the one who'd put out the funds to keep Rowdy off the auction docket? Had she been conspiring with Jo?

It looked like it. But why?

"I had Chance prepare a special meal for you two in the picnic basket in the far corner of the green by the southeast bench," Jo instructed.

Angelica nodded, but not because she'd needed the directions. She already knew where the picnic basket was. She'd been the one *toting* it, for crying out loud. Toby's baby carrier had been left near the basket, as well, and her sedan was parked on the street just beyond the bench.

She should have realized something was off when Jo didn't insist on taking her basket right into the center of the chaos. Jo wasn't the type to live any part of her life on the outskirts. She wanted to dive in and be smack in the middle of everything.

"Talk to each other," Jo suggested in a no-nonsense tone. "Don't let the past eat you up before you figure out where the present is taking you. Work it out. And don't forget to read what is in that envelope."

Then she turned and headed back to the podium without one more word of explanation.

Work *what* out?

Surely Jo should know Rowdy and Ange were far beyond mending fences.

Rowdy growled and yanked at the lasso, pulling it from Ange's hand. He realized only afterward that he'd probably left a rope burn on her palm as he struggled free of the noose, but if Ange noticed she didn't complain or alert him to the fact. It irked him that he felt a moment of remorse for giving her a second's pain.

Not when she'd given him a lifetime's worth.

He stood up to his full six-foot height and straightened his shoulders. He wasn't the tallest man at the auction, but at her five-foot-four-inch frame, he had plenty of height to glower down at her.

His chest burned with fire but his heart incongruously froze solid as anger sluiced through him like an ice storm in Antarctica.

Ange pushed her hoodie back and whipped off her ball cap, shaking her long blond hair out of their confines. Tilting her chin up, she met his gaze head-on.

It wasn't the expression of someone who was sorry for what she'd done. She still maintained the same solitary determination as ever, ready to run roughshod over anyone who stood in her way.

He wouldn't be a sucker twice.

She opened her mouth to speak, but he dug in before she could say a word.

"Ange," he ground out, his low voice sounding like

sandpaper as he leaned back and crossed his arms over his chest, steel walls clamping down around his emotions. No way was he letting her in this time.

"Rowdy," she said, testing his name. She held out a hand to touch his arm but he grunted and twisted away.

But not before he realized she had a baby in her arms.

A *baby*.

"Rowdy," she said again.

His frown deepened at the sound of his name on her lips. It had been such a long time. Her voice was so familiar… and yet, then again, not so much.

He lifted the lasso and shook it under her nose.

"What did you just do?"

Rowdy's eyes briefly settled on the tightly swaddled infant in Ange's arms and then he flicked his gaze to her unadorned left hand. He was reeling with shock to see Ange suddenly back in Serendipity after all this time, especially with a baby in her arms.

Why had she come back?

And why *now*?

She hadn't come home once since the day she'd left him alone and brokenhearted at the altar. She hadn't even bothered to attend her own grandmother's funeral.

And yet now, for no reason Rowdy could guess, she was here, standing in the middle of the community green with a town function going on around her.

Home.

With a baby.

And for some inexplicable reason, she'd somehow finagled things with Jo so she could buy him at auction before the event had even started.

What was with that?

And the craziest thing of all was that she looked

nearly as startled about this whole situation as he felt. As if she didn't know any more than he did about what was happening.

Which couldn't be true, since she'd set it all in motion in the first place.

Hadn't she?

It only remained to be seen as to why. What motive could Ange possibly have to want to see him again?

Or at all.

"I—er—" Ange stammered, shifting from foot to foot and lightly bouncing the baby she cradled in the sling. "What do you mean, what did I do? I didn't do anything."

He gritted his teeth to keep from snapping back at her. He could still turn and walk away, and not one person in town would blame him.

She'd come home for a reason, and it couldn't be anything good. If it was only about selling Granny's ranch to him, well, he and Ange didn't have to talk face-to-face for that. Their Realtors could handle all the details regarding the transaction and all he would have to do would be to sign the papers and fork over the funds to make it a done deal.

Or was it more complicated than that?

Was Jo somehow involved? Jo had purposefully forced their sure-to-be-stormy reunion into pretty much the most public arena possible, leaving Ange and Rowdy no choice but to speak to one another with practically everyone in Serendipity looking on.

And then there was the mysterious letter Jo had given Ange—the one she'd immediately shoved into the back pocket of her jeans.

What was up with that?

Maybe Jo thought Rowdy and Ange ought to bury the hatchet, so to speak, although maybe that wasn't the best metaphor to use in this particular situation.

As if he'd listen to anything *Ange* had to say. She'd ripped his heart to shreds. A reconciliation between the two of them was never going to happen.

Full stop.

Not a relationship. Not a friendship. Nor even acquaintances, as far as he was concerned.

He didn't think he'd ever be able to completely forgive Ange for what she'd done, but he *had* put it all behind him. He'd made his peace and had moved on with his life.

Why dredge it up now?

To be completely honest, Rowdy hadn't been sure *how* he would feel if he ever saw Ange again—or if he'd feel anything at all.

Well, now he knew.

And he didn't like it.

As his past rose to meet him, anger and indignation waged a war in his chest, like dueling pitchforks, parrying back and forth, jabbing sharp points into his heart.

Then he took a breath and the stabbing pains morphed into an ache so deep it left a gaping hole in its wake.

How could merely seeing Ange again so easily stoke to flame all the emotions he'd thought he'd tucked away long ago?

He was an even-keeled man. Not much threw him off-balance one way or the other.

Except for one thing—one person.

Ange had the singular ability to knock him off-kilter.

She'd always been able to do that.

In the past, he'd thought that was a good thing.

Now he knew better.

He remembered his helplessness and hopelessness when he watched her ride off on her horse after their wedding rehearsal—one of the matched set of horses meant for them to depart on after their wedding—leaving him quite literally in the dust.

She hadn't even had the courtesy to look back and wave goodbye.

And now she'd suddenly returned…*why?*

Rowdy was desperately attempting to corral the emotions stampeding through him like a herd of wild buffalo with a pack of wolves on their heels. It took all his effort to keep his voice low so he wouldn't startle the baby.

"What's the deal here, Ange? Why did you buy me at auction?" he whispered, his voice low and raspy.

Her blue eyes widened, her expression sincerely stunned.

Hurt even.

As if she had the right to be.

"Before I answer that question, I think we'd better take Jo's suggestion and head back to where the picnic basket is located. It's not a lot of privacy, but it'll give us a little more than we have standing here. I don't know about you, but I'm not feeling very comfortable right now with everyone's eyes on us and all of them listening to every word we say."

She nodded toward the crowd. True, many had turned back to watch the next bachelor take the stage—the twentysomethings who didn't remember the night Ange had single-handedly ended her tumultuous relationship with Rowdy.

But there were a few furtive glances and murmurs aimed their direction.

Rowdy shrugged. *He* wasn't the one who needed to feel uncomfortable. *He* hadn't done anything wrong. If some of the older townsfolk had long memories, that wasn't on him.

Still, he nodded in agreement and followed her to a bench well out of the main stream of the celebration, where a festive picnic basket bedecked with baby blue pastel ribbons was waiting for hungry picnickers—which Rowdy wasn't. His gut felt like lead.

An infant car seat and a yellow-giraffe-themed diaper bag covered the rest of the bench, marking it out for Rowdy and Ange's use.

Ange picked up the car seat and set it aside on the ground next to the bench, and then did the same thing for the diaper bag, gesturing for him to sit in the space she'd opened.

She remained standing, shifting from foot to foot in a slow, rhythmic rocking motion as she pressed a kiss to the forehead of the infant she was holding in her arms.

"Okay," she said, blowing out a breath. "I have no idea what just happened back there. Though I expect Jo might be able to answer that question, eventually."

"You aren't the one behind this—whatever *this* is? You didn't buy me behind everyone's back?"

"Absolutely not. Why would I do that? I only came to town to settle Granny's estate."

He wasn't sure he believed her, no matter how adamant her refusal. And though he didn't like it, the way she'd worded her statement about not wanting to buy him stung his ego.

"Well, you didn't bother to come to Granny Frances's funeral." He knew it sounded like an accusation, and maybe it was. "So I have to ask myself why you would suddenly show up now."

Pain flashed across her gaze and she shifted her eyes away from him.

"I couldn't come," she murmured.

He waited for more of an explanation, but none appeared to be forthcoming.

"Can you hold the baby for a minute while I set things up?" she asked, pressing the infant into the crook of his arm before waiting for his answer.

"Uh. Yeah. Sure," he said, seconds after the fact.

He shifted uncomfortably. He didn't know how to hold a baby—at least a human infant—and he felt like an awkward giant made of all thumbs. His gut churned.

He was used to bottle-feeding little lambs, and this tiny bundle of humanity lying in the crook of his arm was a whole other thing entirely.

"His name is Toby." Ange's rich alto was warm and filled with pride and wonder when she spoke of her son. "Toby Francis, after Granny."

Rowdy pushed the pastel green receiving blanket off the baby's forehead so he could see his face better, and a jolt of realization slashed through him.

Toby was…

Ange hadn't said…

"Yes," she affirmed in a whisper, reading the recognition in his eyes. "Toby has Down syndrome."

Rowdy's throat tightened. He was even less familiar with Down syndrome than he was with babies in general, but while this little guy was alert he wasn't fussy, and after a moment, Rowdy's heart calmed.

"He's beautiful," he said, and meant it.

Rowdy brushed a finger over Toby's silky white-blond hair, a shade lighter than his mother's. His almond-shaped blue eyes had popped open at the sound of Rowdy's deep voice and were now staring up at him with interest. The little guy's mouth was nearly wide enough to fit his entire tiny fist, and he was loudly sucking on his knuckles.

Ange's eyes widened at Rowdy's compliment, as if she didn't hear kind remarks very often. And maybe she didn't. People were strange when it came to anything or anyone different than they were.

Special needs freaked some people out, but it didn't bother Rowdy. As far as he was concerned, all humans carried the same dignity because they were made in the image of God. Different was beautiful.

She smiled sincerely, apparently satisfied that he meant what he said.

Rowdy *always* meant what he said.

"I know, right?" she whispered after a moment. "He's such a sweetheart. The biggest blessing in my life."

As little as Rowdy knew about babies, his being a perennial bachelor, he knew enough to realize infants were a challenge for any new mama or daddy, even the experienced ones. He'd watched all of his friends get married and have babies, and seen their slow adjustments to the learning curve called parenting.

Rowdy's closest friend, Danny Lockhart, complained nonstop about having to stay up all night with a fussy infant who had her days and nights mixed up—and then in the next breath he'd proudly show her off, forgetting whatever trials he faced at two o'clock in the morning.

So it seemed strange to Rowdy that Ange would choose to return to Serendipity, where she had no real support as a single mother. Her parents had moved away long ago, not that they were ever terribly supportive of her. And he doubted, given the past, that Ange had many friends here, either, as horrible as that was to think.

Was Toby's father in the picture?

If so, where was he? Holding down the fort in Denver while Ange visited Serendipity?

She didn't have a ring on her finger. Rowdy didn't have much use for men who didn't marry the woman they intended to start a family with.

But that was a discussion for another time.

Rowdy had so many questions that he didn't even know where to begin.

As Ange prepared the picnic lunch, Rowdy studied her face. The telltale dark circles under her eyes and the lines of stress creasing her brow suggested her life hadn't been easy on her.

She looked older than her twenty-nine years, but she was nonetheless beautiful enough to make Rowdy's stomach flip as he attempted to rein in the physical attraction he'd always felt toward her.

That much, at least, hadn't changed. He'd always seen the inherent beauty in her that she didn't see when she looked in the mirror.

But it was the *only* thing that hadn't changed. And he had no idea what she saw when she looked in the mirror these days.

"How's Toby doing?" she asked as she popped the top on a can of Rowdy's favorite soda.

"Sleeping again. He's really cute. Still sucking his fist, even when he's napping."

Ange handed Rowdy the soda and took Toby into

her arms, landing a soft kiss on his cheek before gently placing him in his car seat so she and Rowdy would have their hands free to eat.

"Still your favorite?" she asked, gesturing toward his soda can.

He lifted the can in salute. "I'm surprised you remembered."

Another flash of pain crossed her gaze. "I remember a lot, if truth be told."

So did he.

And he really, *really* wished he didn't. Because with every unexpected glimpse into their past, every unanticipated memory, it became harder and harder to catch a breath.

He hadn't been ready to see Ange again.

And he wasn't sure he ever would be.

Chapter Two

Angelica settled cross-legged on the bench next to Rowdy and set her plate in her lap.

"It isn't just the soda." He gestured with his fork to incorporate all the food on his plate. "This is my favorite meal—barbecued pork ribs, fried okra and mashed potatoes in a thick brown gravy."

"The meal was my suggestion, but I can't take credit for the cooking. I can't cook a thing. On my own, I subsist on deli chicken and pizza made from spaghetti sauce and cheese toasted on a slice of bread."

It only now struck her, as she was going on and on about her usual diet—which Rowdy could probably not care less about—that she had unconsciously asked for Rowdy's favorite meal when Jo had asked her what to pack for the picnic today.

Her breath hitched. All these years, and Rowdy's favorites had still come to mind.

"This delicious meal is all straight from Cup O' Jo's. Chance cooked the food and Jo packed and decorated the picnic basket."

"A baby theme? Clever."

"It's cute," she agreed. "Will you please say grace for us before we start the meal?"

His fork clattered to his plate as he gaped at her in astonishment.

Angelica wasn't surprised by his response. She had grown up a PK—a preacher's kid. Back when she and Rowdy were dating, she was as rebellious as the day was long and wanted nothing to do with church.

Or God.

That had all changed the day she found out she was pregnant with Toby. Suddenly God was very real to her. How else could she explain the tiny human being fearfully and wonderfully formed within her womb?

When she'd told Josh, the father of her child, about their baby, he had scoffed at her, called her horrible names and insisted the child wasn't his. When he walked out the door, he had walked out of her life. And good riddance to him.

Josh had known he was the only man in her life, the only man she had been with ever, because she had only given in to him after months of pressure. But he hadn't wanted to accept the responsibility of fatherhood or the effects it would have on his freewheeling lifestyle. He didn't want to be tied down with a family.

So he'd simply denied the truth and disappeared.

In a way, Angelica felt she deserved that rejection and in the long run God had been looking out for her. It was better for her and her baby not to have been permanently locked into what had never been a healthy relationship to begin with.

God alone had been her constant companion after Josh had left her. She had a few work acquaintances from the high-end hotel in which she was a white-gloved banquet server, but by throwing herself into Denver's nightlife she'd never made any real connections, and she'd let those few friendships lapse when she'd started dating Josh.

Angelica pulled her thoughts from the past and focused her attention on Rowdy.

"I know what you're probably thinking. Have I really changed, or am I just trying to unsettle you by asking you to say grace?"

His gaze widened and then his brow furrowed, a frown gathering on his lips. He put his plate aside.

"You said it, not me."

Toby stirred and Ange set her uneaten food aside to scoop him into her arms. She shuffled through the diaper bag until she found a bottle of formula, giving it a good shake to make sure it was well mixed.

"Discovering I was pregnant with Toby changed my world," she said, glancing up at Rowdy. "And I mean all of it. I realize I've made a lot of mistakes in my past. I've hurt people—"

Her gaze dropped to Rowdy's hands. He was clenching the edge of the bench until his knuckles turned white.

She felt bad for him, but unlike with Josh, she had no fear of him losing his temper. Unless time had completely changed him, he wasn't a man who would fly off the handle. He was self-controlled and even tempered, even with the woman who had broken his heart.

"Hurt *you*," she finished, swallowing hard.

His muscles tightened until his shoulders visibly rippled with tension, and her own stress increased.

"Is this some kind of twelve-step program or some-thing? You're here because you have to make amends?"

"What? No. I'm here to pay respects to Granny, since I was having Toby on the day she passed away. That, and to settle the estate. I already know there is nothing I can do or say that would change how you think about me and what I did to you."

Angelica knew her words alone would mean noth-ing to the man sitting next to her on the bench, the man she'd once loved with all her heart and who had once loved her. He had been prepared to commit his life to her.

He would never know how much she'd sacrificed, and all because she'd loved him.

Toby batted the bottle in her hand, reminding her that she had a hungry boy to feed.

"I'm sorry. There you go, sweetheart," she mur-mured, pressing the bottle to Toby's lips.

"He's a noisy eater," Rowdy observed, apparently deciding to keep their conversation at a casual level for the time being.

"He sometimes has trouble latching on and getting his lips where they need to be to get good suction."

"Because he has Down syndrome?"

Ange nodded, but she wasn't dismayed by the fact. Toby was just Toby, her son. "Every day is a new ad-venture with this little guy."

"And your parents? How do they like their new grandson? They must be proud."

"They don't know about him yet," she admitted, her heart clenching and heat rising to her face. "You prob-ably know that they left the parish here in Serendipity for a small town in Wyoming shortly after I left town.

"My dad pretty much disowned me when I acted so awfully to you in such a public way, because in his mind my actions rubbed off on him. And I guess in a way he is right about that. I was the reason he took a new pastorate far away from Serendipity. I've tried reaching out to Mom, but she doesn't dare cross him, not even for my sake."

"So, you don't see them then?"

"No. Not at all."

He shook his head. "That's a shame."

"It is." She shook her head. "It's frustrating, but I take full responsibility for my own actions. I don't like to see my family torn apart, but I can't blame them for distancing themselves from me."

She scoffed. "I thought I was so worldly, leaving Serendipity behind and going off on my own, but in truth, I was way out of my element from the day I got to Denver. A preacher's kid from a small town? I had no idea what I was getting into and was practically swallowed alive. At first, I didn't want to stay at all.

"But of course, there were even more reasons I couldn't come home—er, back to Serendipity—when things in Denver didn't turn out like I'd planned. Not after…well…"

His eyes snapped to hers. She held his gaze but then had to look away for a moment as guilt flooded through her.

With a deep breath, she returned her gaze to his.

"Obviously, I had no intention of seeing you today. But here we are."

"Here we are," he repeated. He narrowed his eyes on her. "So now what?"

* * *

Rowdy's emotions were run ragged and frankly, he had had enough. It was all he could do not to bolt from the scene like a skittish lamb.

He lifted his bruised and battered heart to the Lord. *God, help me.*

A short, concise prayer that said it all.

Ange had returned to Serendipity, no longer the pretty girl with a chip on her shoulder who he'd once known and loved, but a striking, mature woman—and a mother with a newborn baby who had seen her share of rough times.

She hadn't said anything about Toby's father, but Rowdy knew better than to make any assumptions.

Right now, he just hurt, a relentless ache that started in his heart and radiated through his limbs.

"The envelope," Ange said, digging into her back pocket. "Maybe that will give us a clue."

He raised his brows. "A clue to what?"

"What we're supposed to be talking about. Jo slipped me an envelope when she handed me the—er—lariat. It's from Granny and addressed to both of us. The first one only had my name on it."

"There are more than one?"

Ange sniffed softly. "Believe me, I wouldn't be wandering around in public if I'd had any choice in the matter."

"I don't understand."

"Yeah, me neither, exactly. I only came to town to pay my respects and get the sale started on Granny's ranch."

"So, you are selling, then?"

Her gaze widened. "Of course. What on earth would I do with a sheep farm?"

"I'm an interested buyer, you know."

She nodded. "I figured. But I also assumed I could take care of the estate and the paperwork without actually having to see you—" Her words skidded. "I mean, any potential buyers. Instead, I'm out and about at a packed town function. Which is exactly where I don't want to be. Especially not making the kind of scene I ended up making. I absolutely didn't have any intention of seeing you again."

"So why are you here, then?"

"The letter in the first envelope had very specific instructions. It was addressed to me from Granny. Jo said that Granny would understand if I wanted to sell the ranch, but that she requested I follow the instructions in the envelope. Kind of like a last wish, I guess."

"And that said…?"

"Picnic With Jo."

"That's it?"

"That's it."

"Wow. That's about as vague as it gets. But Jo knew a lot more about what Granny was asking than you did. And she didn't even hint about what you were walking into?"

"Not one word. She must have been busting up inside not being able to tell me anything."

"So you didn't know anything about the auction being today? Or, most especially, about buying me at auction before the event even got off the ground?"

"No, but Jo certainly did. And so, I think, did Granny. Before she passed on, she requested that I visit her on this particular weekend. I'm wondering if she wanted me to attend this auction all along, even if she'd still been here to come with me."

"You think we've been set up?"

Ange frowned and nodded, looking none too pleased by the thought.

"But why?"

She shrugged. "Your guess is as good as mine. Maybe Granny wanted to make sure the sale of the ranch went smoothly."

"That doesn't feel like enough of an explanation. We didn't have to meet at the auction to work out the details of our real estate transaction. And why go to all the trouble of the cryptic letter? Why not just spell it all out?" he asked.

Ange held up the second envelope, which Rowdy could now clearly see had both of their names scrawled on it.

"I have no idea. Here's hoping this one will tell us exactly where we're supposed to go from here."

Toby worked the bottle from his mouth with a gurgle and Angelica shifted him to her shoulder.

She pushed the envelope in Rowdy's direction. "I guess we won't know until we open it. Why don't you do the honors, since I've got my hands full?"

Rowdy plucked the envelope from her grasp and gingerly opened it, unfolding the single tri-folded sheet of typing paper. He wasn't sure he even wanted to be any part of this, but Granny Frances, as she'd insisted he call her back when he was a teenage boy dating her granddaughter, had been a huge influence in his life. He couldn't let her down now.

She was a stubborn woman who'd continued to manage her ranch for as long as possible, saying it gave her great joy to be with her animals and her pain wasn't going to keep her down.

But eventually, it had become too hard even for one as strong and stoic as Granny Frances.

In her final weeks, when she'd gotten too sick to care for herself, much less her flock, on her own, a palliative care nurse had come to look out for Granny Frances and Rowdy had stepped in and done the ranch work for her.

In reality, at this point he was already running Granny Frances's ranch as if it was his own. As long as another buyer with deep pockets didn't sweep in, which wasn't likely in a town as small as Serendipity, it was just a matter of signing the papers to make the land his legally as well as practically.

His gaze quickly took in the words on Granny's missive and he shook his head.

If they were expecting answers, this letter didn't contain them.

These words were, in fact, the exact opposite.

"Feed My Sheep."

Three words in Granny Frances's handwriting.

Three lousy words.

"Great," Ange groaned. "Another cryptic note. What do you suppose this one means?"

Rowdy ran a hand across the stubble on his jaw. "It sounds like something out of the Holy Scriptures. You know, when Jesus was speaking to Peter and kept telling him to feed his sheep? You think this is some kind of secret message?"

"I don't know. I'm not even certain Granny was lucid when she wrote this stuff down. Maybe what she really meant to convey didn't quite translate to paper."

Rowdy hoped that was the case, but he sincerely

doubted it. Life was never that simple, and he'd been there during Granny Frances's final days. She had been coherent until her very last moments, when she had given her soul up to Jesus.

"No, I don't think so," he said. "Whatever this letter means, she knew what she was doing when she wrote it. I'm sorry you weren't able to be there with her during her last moments, but I was, and I can tell you definitively that she was fully lucid all the way up to the end."

His words weren't quite the accusation they had been earlier. "The last word she breathed was *Jesus*. Her expression was so peaceful. There is absolutely no doubt in my mind her Savior was there waiting with open arms to welcome her into heaven."

Tears sprang to Ange's eyes and she dashed them back with her palm, while her face blotched with red and purple. Rowdy thought she might be having trouble holding herself together. She'd always been a private person and her struggle with grief was real, even if everything else she'd ever told him varied from the truth in some way.

And the worst part was, seeing her tears tore at him, ripping into his chest.

He didn't know how he felt about her expressing her grief. When Ange had left Serendipity, it had been for good. She had not even come to visit Granny Frances.

Not once.

And though he now understood why she had missed Granny's funeral, that didn't make the whole situation any less confusing.

Here she was now, trying to make things right when it was too late for her to do so.

Too late for Granny Frances.

And too late for him.

For *them*.

He swallowed hard, but a smile lingered on his lips despite the fresh wave of grief.

He stammered quickly over his next sentence, returning the conversation to safer grounds.

"J-Jo appeared to know exactly what was going on," he pointed out. "Maybe we should just toss the letter and ask her straight out. I'll bet she has answers."

"Oh, I intend to," Ange assured him.

"Although how much she'll divulge is another thing entirely. If she made a pact with Granny Frances, we are only going to learn what your granny wanted us to know."

"That's right. So I guess we have to play sleuth and see if we can figure it out on our own before we approach Jo on the matter."

"Well, the first note was literal, right?" he asked, trying to make logic out of the cryptic words. *"Picnic With Jo?"*

"Up to a point, it was. Obviously, there was a lot Granny left out. Intentionally, I suspect."

"So, what if this letter is the same? Maybe she really means you should feed her sheep."

"Me? I don't know the first thing about sheep." Her gaze widened and for a moment, she gaped at him. "There aren't any *sheep* at her ranch anymore, are there? She adored her sheep. I remember she used to lovingly refer to them as her woolies. She wouldn't let them starve. I guess I just assumed that since Granny knew she had a terminal disease, she'd have all her affairs in order and sell her stock off before she passed."

He bit on the inside of his cheek, wondering just how much he ought to tell her.

Any way he looked at it, Rowdy didn't like where this was going. The way he saw it, and the only interpretation that made any sense, was that Granny Frances's intention was for him to subtly introduce Ange to the ins and outs of ranch life, possibly hoping she'd decide to keep the land in the family.

But that was unfair, for so many reasons. For one thing, Ange was the furthest thing from a rancher ever, and she'd need a ton of help—assistance Granny Frances assumed would come from Rowdy.

And for another, though Granny Frances knew he had taken over her ranch out of love for her, she also had to have known he needed to expand if he was going to keep making a profit on his land.

They had never spoken about it, but joining their two ranches was the perfect answer to that dilemma. She would have had to have been blind not to recognize the hope he carried in his heart for the joining of the properties, and Granny Frances was as astute a woman as one could find anywhere.

"I've been taking care of her stock," he admitted, his thoughts working frantically.

Ange looked mortified. "You don't really think she wants you to teach me how to care for *sheep*, do you?"

He shrugged.

It crossed his mind that he could sabotage the plans to get Ange on board to keep the ranch, if that was what they were. After all, Ange deciding to do so was the exact opposite of what Rowdy wanted to happen.

But deep down, Rowdy knew he would never be so underhanded as to resort to anything as devious as that.

It wasn't in his nature. Nor would God be happy with that kind of thinking—much less acting.

Besides, as far as he knew, Ange still agreed with him about how Granny Frances's estate should be handled—so there should be no conflict despite Granny Frances's note suggesting that Ange needed to learn to feed the sheep.

No. Ange wanted to sell her ranch.

To him.

And he wanted to buy.

It was a win-win, putting enough money in her pocket to find a good place to live in the city and have some left over for Toby's long-term care.

It wasn't that he was afraid Ange would change her mind and decide to stick around. Ranch work was hard and dusty. If anything, *Feed My Sheep* would convince her that she should sell like nothing else might.

Even one day of herding sheep and mucking around in a smelly barn would be enough to send her running back to Denver faster than she could say "Giddyap." He would put his last nickel on the fact that she didn't even own a pair of mud boots.

And he *had* loved Granny Frances. That fact was cut-and-dried. If teaching Ange to feed Granny's sheep would honor the deceased's memory, then he would cowboy up and do it, even if every second in her presence was torture, plain and simple.

He just had to hold on to the knowledge that it wouldn't last forever. Whatever the outcome of this game Granny Frances was playing with them, it would end eventually.

He would hold fast to the idea that Ange had indicated she wanted to sell him the ranch. The sooner he cooperated with this—whatever *this* was—the sooner she would leave and he could take full ownership of Granny Frances's ranch and incorporate it into his own.

"You don't think—" Ange started, and then her sentence dropped off and her face drained of color. "This is the second envelope. Jo didn't say it was the *last* one. What if there are more letters after this one? More stuff she wants us to do, more riddles we have to figure out? Could this be some kind of outrageous scavenger hunt Granny is sending us on?"

Oh, no, no, no, no, no, no, no.

Rowdy shook his head voraciously as his thoughts denied the possibility.

"I don't think we ought to keep speculating on this bit. We need to go find Jo and clear up the confusion," he said. "There's no question that I want to honor Granny Frances's memory, but…"

"Exactly," she said, even though he hadn't finished his sentence. "Whatever needs doing, needs doing quickly. I absolutely cannot stick around after this weekend. My flight back to Denver leaves tomorrow afternoon. I've got to return to my job on Monday. It's my first day back after my maternity leave. I'll lose my position for sure if I don't show up. My boss is a real stickler about stuff like that."

"What do you do?"

"I work in a five-star hotel as part of the dining staff for large, catered events. I'm one of those white-gloved banquet servers you encounter when you go to large meetings at a hotel. We have a lot of major corporations that come through, as well as conventions that meet there."

"Sounds interesting."

"Not really. It's a lot of standing and people can get really snooty. But it pays the bills, and I can't afford to be picky. I'm not going to have the money to pay anything if I don't get back there on time. Oh, the joys of living from paycheck to paycheck."

Rowdy didn't know about that. He lived from season to season.

"How old is Toby?" Rowdy asked, as what Ange had said earlier suddenly clicked. She had indicated she'd missed Granny Frances's funeral because she was in the hospital having Toby, but that was only three weeks ago.

"Three weeks," Ange confirmed.

"Don't you get maternity leave for twelve weeks?" He had no idea where he'd pulled that information from. A television show, maybe. But it sounded fair enough.

She scoffed softly. "In the best of all worlds. I'm allowed to take twelve weeks, but my checkbook can't handle the money I'd lose. Now I have Toby to support. I can't afford to take off a whole twelve weeks. Three was pushing it."

Rowdy didn't know if Granny Frances had left Ange any money in her will, but it occurred to him that if they could get this deal done with the real estate, that would give Ange something to ease her load.

"Let's talk to Jo and see what we can do. The sooner, the better. It's possible that we will be able to work out some of the details about me buying Granny Frances's ranch, which would in turn save you the trouble of having to come back to Serendipity."

Her face reddened. "Pushy, much?"

He scowled and shook his head. He was trying to be nice and she was taking it all the wrong way.

"That's not what I meant. Am I mistaken? I thought that selling the ranch was what you wanted to do."

She sighed. "It is. I just don't like feeling as if you are corralling me out of town. You don't have to be brash about it. I get the hint."

She shook her head. "Don't worry. We'll just have to set aside the whole *Feed My Sheep* thing and let Jo know that we aren't going to continue. Surely, it can't be so important that we have to drop our entire lives to pursue it."

"Maybe not," he admitted.

"Well, like I said, I have to be on a plane tomorrow afternoon anyway, so I can't keep playing this peculiar game even if I wanted to."

She smiled, but Rowdy could see the trouble she was having in curling her lips upward. "You'll be happy to know that I'll be out of your life tomorrow—and you'll never have to see me again."

Chapter Three

True to her word, Angelica took Toby and left Serendipity the next day. But by Friday afternoon, she had returned to her hometown without the slightest idea of what she was going to do next.

She had been telling the truth when she'd informed Rowdy that she didn't plan to pop back up in town anytime soon—or ever—but once in Denver she'd found that she couldn't set her time in Serendipity and with Rowdy aside as easily as all that.

In her heart of hearts, she wasn't sure she had done the right thing by returning to the big city and proceeding with selling Granny's ranch.

Not for herself, and not for Toby.

The whole envelope-deliveries-and-cryptic-messages thing felt like unfinished business. She'd left town without fulfilling Granny's request, and that really bothered her.

She hadn't fed any sheep yet.

Instead, she'd run away from the obligation. Just as she'd done before.

When the going got tough, Angelica bolted.

It was her modus operandi.

She hated to think that after all this time and experience, she hadn't changed. Worse yet, what she did affected Toby.

Was Toby really better off in Denver? Or was she just trying to take the easy way out?

No. She couldn't repeat her mistakes.

Not again.

Not even knowing Rowdy wouldn't be thrilled to see her. She'd simply have to explain her reasons for returning and hope he'd understand.

And she didn't even want to think about how the rest of the town would perceive her return, particularly driving a moving van filled with what little furniture she had, with her car hooked up behind.

Maybe that was part of the reason she had to go back. To prove to herself *and* the people of Serendipity that she had changed. That she was no longer the rebellious teenager and young adult, but that the Lord had touched her heart and altered her world. And that becoming a mother to Toby had made a substantial difference, as well.

She was putting Toby's crib together in the guest bedroom, Toby gurgling in the bouncer by her side, when the doorbell rang. She started in surprise.

She wasn't expecting anyone.

"Guess I'd better get that, yeah, little man?"

She moved Toby, bouncer and all, into the living room and opened the door to find a beaming Jo on the other side, her arms laden with a large box of prepared casserole dishes.

"What is all this?" she asked.

"You should have told me you were coming back," Jo

chided, weaseling through the door and into the house without waiting for an invitation. "I had to hear it from the three old men that sit in their rockers outside Emerson's Hardware. They said they saw a moving van passing through and I knew it would be you."

Angelica didn't ask how she had known.

"I'm sure you have more than enough to do getting your furniture into Frances's ranch house all on your own. Give me an hour and I can round up some fellows to do the heavy lifting for you."

"Oh, no. That's okay. I've got most of it already done—or at least what I need for now. I had no use for the furniture I was using in my small apartment in Denver, so I sold it off. I've already unloaded everything I need for Toby."

She relieved Jo of the box of food, which was surprisingly heavy, and placed it on the kitchen counter.

"What is all this?"

Jo chuckled with glee.

"I simply mentioned to some of the ladies of the church that you'd been seen entering town with your moving van, and before I knew it, casseroles were coming in right and left."

Tears burned in Angelica's eyes.

"But I—I—" she stammered.

This was the last thing she'd imagined would happen—her neighbors, especially anyone from the church, offering their support.

"I know what you're thinking, dear." Jo wrapped her in a motherly bear hug. "It's going to be okay. Let it go, honey."

Try as she might, Angelica could no longer hold in her grief. This act of charity from people who had every reason to turn their backs on her broke her emotional dam wide. Sorrow for all she had lost, and all the mistakes she had made, flooded out of her. Jo simply patted her back and made quiet, reassuring shushing noises.

At length, she had no tears left to cry. She pulled back and brushed the tears from her eyes with her palms.

"I'm sorry for blubbering all over you," she said with a hiccup.

"That's what I'm here for, dear. Anytime you need a hug, or just to talk, I'm your woman."

"I know."

"So, it looks like you're moving in, then." It wasn't a question. In fact, Jo sounded as if it had been her idea in the first place.

"I am. I decided I needed to finish what I started here. I need some time to figure out what I'm going to do next."

"What about your job in Denver? Are you taking a leave of absence?"

Angelica laughed, but it sounded more like a snort.

"My boss at the hotel was none too crazy to hear I needed to be in Serendipity to work out the wrinkles in Granny's estate. I believe his exact words were, 'Don't expect a reference.'"

"Oh, no, dear. I'm so sorry."

"It's for the best. I had hoped for better, since I gave him the news face-to-face, but I suppose I can't blame him. When I asked for extended leave without notice, I put him short one banquet server, and the hotel was hosting a dinner for an enormous Fortune 500 company conference that was arriving for the weekend."

"He'll live. Sometimes ya just gotta do what ya gotta do."

"Truthfully, I'm relieved to be rid of the high-stress job. Trying to keep the dishes flowing and the diners happy while management constantly looked over my shoulder isn't my idea of a good time, but I managed to get by on the wages I earned, at least until Toby came into my life."

"Babies are expensive," Jo said. "Diapers, clothes, supplement formula. And that's to say nothing of his crib and car seat."

"So true." Angelica had shifted most of her food budget to covering Toby's needs, and there were many days when she only ate one meal. Not ideal for a nursing mother.

But Granny's passing had changed everything, and Angelica knew Granny would be happy she had given her granddaughter a way out of the rat race, even if it wasn't quite what Granny had in mind.

A sheep farmer she was not.

Still—that was that.

Her job in Denver, such that it was, no longer existed. She had severed her last ties to the big city and would be able to make decisions based on what was best for her and Toby, no matter where she decided to live and what she decided to do in the end.

Maybe, with the money Granny had left her along with the sale of the ranch, she could go to school and become—

Well, she didn't know *what* she wanted to become, only that an overglorified waitress wasn't it.

"I'd like to try to figure out my own head and heart in the slower pace of Serendipity while I stay here at Granny's ranch."

"That's exactly what Frances wanted to provide for you," Jo assured her.

Angelica knew she was facing a whole new set of challenges if she was going to follow Granny's directive—how to feed sheep, for one thing.

How a ranch made a profit. Or what she might be able to get by selling the land to Rowdy.

What the messages in the envelopes meant.

And where the paper trail or scavenger hunt or whatever Granny had considered it would end.

"About this *Feed My Sheep* thing," Angelica asked. "Am I supposed to be learning how to feed Granny's sheep, or am I missing the point? And how many envelopes are there, anyway?"

"All I can say is you're on the right track. And you can expect more from Frances when the time is right. These letters are your granny's last wishes to you. It was her fervent prayer that you and Rowdy would follow her instructions."

Angelica didn't know about Rowdy, but she couldn't find it in her heart to deny Granny what she wanted. Not when she had missed Granny's final days and even her funeral.

In good faith, what else could she do?

"I'll get out of your hair, then. You holler if you need anything." Jo patted Angelica's arm and leaned down to kiss Toby on the forehead before letting herself out, disappearing as quickly as she had appeared.

Jo left Angelica with much to think about. It seemed that Granny had known all along that Angelica would need time after becoming a mother to work out what she wanted to do with her life, to see her future with more clarity.

Granny was the one person in Serendipity—well, one of two, if Angelica counted Granny's bosom friend Jo—who knew how hard Angelica's life had been after leaving town.

Angelica would follow Granny's directives, but she didn't know what good it would do. How would hanging out with a bunch of smelly sheep, not to mention the hodgepodge of other animals Granny raised, give her a better idea of what she should be doing with her life?

The pungent aroma of country living might clear out her nostrils, but it would hardly clear her head.

Still, she *had* experienced a moment of homecoming when she'd taken what little she and Toby owned and moved it into the sprawling ranch home. She had settled into one of the spare bedrooms across from where Granny used to sleep, and had arranged a small nursery in the other.

Granny's one-level ranch house was as country inside as out, with wooden furniture, homemade quilts and the scent of evergreen from the wood-burning stove Granny had used to heat her home.

Living at Granny's, at least, would be peaceful and a happy reminder of the past spent with her favorite relative. Not having to pay rent was a huge boon, as well, since she'd dropped her month-to-month lease apartment in Denver.

But balancing that with the amount of work she would have to do to keep the ranch going tipped the scales the other direction. She was overwhelmed by the mere thought of trying to do all that and care for her special needs son, too.

How was she supposed to take care of the animals? Rowdy had said the sheep were in the far pasture, and she'd seen the coop of chickens on her way in. The hay fields would be ripe for harvesting come fall. She would have to learn how to herd the flock with the two border collies and ascertain just how Granny's Anatolian shepherd guarded the flock at night. At this point she didn't even know their names. Granny had always taken the border collies inside with her at night. Even as unfamiliar as she was with dogs, Angelica couldn't help but think she ought to do the same thing.

She wondered if Granny's old mare was still stabled on the ranch. And then there was shearing the sheep and gathering the chickens' eggs and who knew what other chores awaited her?

She had a new appreciation for Granny, who had done it all herself after Angelica's grandfather had died twenty years ago. Granny brought in a few men to harvest her hay crop, but other than that she was a one-woman talent show.

The sheep, the dogs, the chickens—that was all her.

Angelica didn't feel nearly up to the task. It was all she could do just to learn to be a mama to Toby. It gave her pause once again to wonder if she'd made a mistake coming back here.

She finished setting up the crib and left a message for Rowdy on his answering machine to let him know she was back in town to take care of the whole *Feed My Sheep* business, as dubious as that was. And the longer she waited for him to return her call, the more she wondered what in the world she thought she was doing.

If Rowdy wasn't the man in question, she would suspect he might not call back at all, that he might be avoiding her on purpose. But it *was* Rowdy, and he wasn't the kind of person to be intentionally unkind, even if it was to the woman who held the town record on heart-lessness.

Now that she was back in the hometown she'd never thought to see again, and waiting on the man she'd once left at the altar—it all felt surreal and it made her a little sick to her stomach.

What was she really doing here, anyway?

She folded a basket full of Toby's clothes while she waited for Rowdy to return her message, but instead of phoning he showed up on her doorstep, the second un-expected visitor of the day, covered with a day's worth of dirt and grime and smelling cowboy fresh.

Definitely not the most romantic scent in the world, by any means, but the combination of old leather and outdoor living was inexplicably appealing to Angelica, at least on Rowdy.

And the all-male smell of him tripped memories long hidden, reminding her of old times in a way she'd rather not think about.

When they were happy together.

Before everything had gone south.

"Rowdy," Angelica exclaimed in surprise, shifting Toby to the crook of her arm. "You didn't have to come over. I just wanted to touch base with you and let you know I was back in town."

"No bother. I come over every afternoon to care for Granny Frances's stock, anyway."

Of course he did.

It wasn't just the sheep. Angelica wondered why she hadn't thought of it before. She hadn't toured the ranch yet, but it wasn't falling down around her and all of the animals she'd seen looked healthy.

Animals that couldn't possibly be there unless someone was caring for them.

Duh!

Someone would have had to take over for Granny when she became too ill to work.

Who else but Rowdy, the friendly young rancher next door, and one of the only men in town who knew how to properly care for a sheep farm?

And he'd clearly continued after Granny had passed.

Angelica's heart sank.

She had no idea how to care for sheep—hence, she suspected, the letter from Granny with Rowdy's name on it as well as her own.

Rowdy was the one man who could truly help her. And the man who had the most to gain from continuing to work the stock, assuming she would be selling both the land and animals to him.

The sooner she got the hang of this, the sooner she could send Rowdy on his way—or he could send her on hers. She was so confused and grieving she couldn't see up from down.

At the very least, if Rowdy showed her how to feed Granny's sheep they would both be able to move on to whatever was in the next envelope. Jo hadn't said how many they were to expect, but Angelica had to believe they were near the end of this crazy chase.

She gestured Rowdy inside. Without a word, he hung his hat on a peg near the door and removed his boots, placing them on the mat next to the hat rack, just as Granny had always insisted he do when Rowdy and Angelica were dating as teenagers.

Her throat burned with grief at the memory and she had to blink back the tears that pricked against the backs of her eyes. Rowdy was the same cowboy he'd been back then. The only difference now was time, distance and the slight limp in his left leg.

And Granny was gone.

Her bright personality that always lit up the atmosphere had disappeared, leaving Angelica's heart dim.

She mentally shook herself. Now wasn't the time for her to break down. She'd done that enough with Jo, and besides, Granny wouldn't want her to spend her days crying. She saved her grief—for Granny, for Rowdy and for the way her life had turned out—for the middle of the night when she was nursing Toby. Her sweet little baby was the only person who could soothe her as she offered tears and whispered prayers into the darkness.

Rowdy hesitated until she'd taken a seat on the rocker before he propped himself on the edge of the couch, clutching his hands in front of him and leaning his forearms on his knees, his gaze on the carefully polished hardwood floor.

She wondered if he was trying to gather his thoughts to say something, but when he didn't speak, Angelica jumped in with the first question that came to mind.

"How much has Granny been paying you?"

His head popped up and his gaze widened in astonishment.

"What?"

"You must have been doing all the chores around here for quite some time. I assume Granny gave you something for all the help you've been to her."

He frowned. "You really think I would do a thing like that to Granny Frances? Ask her to pay me something when she was on her deathbed? That would be a horrible way to treat a friend."

The sound that emerged from deep in his chest was very much like a growl.

"Wow. You really have a bad opinion of me, don't you? It makes me wonder why you ever agreed to marry me in the first place, if you think I'm that kind of man," Rowdy said. "Then again, I guess when push came to shove you weren't much on follow through, now, were you?"

His barbed words and resentful tone caught on to Angelica's tight nerves and yanked at them, but as much as she wanted to, she didn't bite back.

What good would it serve?

And anyway, he was right.

He shrugged. "I did what had to be done. Out here in the country it's called being neighborly. Maybe you forgot about that after all your years in the city."

"No need to be touchy," she said, trying to keep her voice even for Toby's sake. "It's just that taking over all the chores for the entire ranch, despite its small size, is a tremendous thing to ask, even of a man with as much integrity as you have. Especially since you have—" she gestured toward his bad knee "—health issues. I can't imagine it's easy for you."

"Then don't bother yourself about it." He frowned in objection. "My knee rarely hurts anymore. And it doesn't stop me from doing my job. Ever."

She held her hands up in surrender.

He narrowed his eyes on her, taking her measure. She met and held his gaze.

She no doubt came up wanting in his eyes. But that wouldn't be news to Rowdy.

"Granny Frances wanted to pay me," he finally admitted. "I wouldn't let her."

Angelica nodded. That sounded like Granny. Likewise, it sounded just exactly like Rowdy.

"I don't have much to offer. The money Granny left me is enough for me to live on for a few months, but not enough to pay for a ranch hand to help me."

She shrugged. "Frankly, without you, there's no way I'm going to be able to take care of all these animals. I know I'm not Granny. Not even close. I can't do it all." She paused. "Although maybe that's to your advantage. The sooner I fail, the sooner you get Granny's ranch."

"I'm not going to sit here and tell you I don't want this ranch. You know I do. My own ranch is barely keeping up with the cost of inflation. The extra land and stock will be just the shot in the arm I need."

"I figured."

"But as far as you failing this test, if that's what it is, I don't think that's what Granny Frances had on her mind," he said thoughtfully. "Why was her letter addressed to both of us if she didn't really want me to give you a hand? She even specifically mentioned the sheep. And anyway, if I am going to eventually own this place—and I've already put it all out on the table and admitted that's what I want in the end—I'd rather keep the ranch in shape than have to do extra work getting everything back in order after the land becomes mine."

Angelica brushed a long strand of hair behind her ear and shifted Toby to her other shoulder. "I'm willing to accept your help, for Granny's sake, but I realize this is asking a lot of both of us. There is one obvious factor we haven't really talked about. She is pushing us together for a reason."

He grunted in agreement and threaded his fingers through his thick blond curls.

"Can we really get along well enough to work together after—well, everything? Because to be honest, I'm not sure that can happen no matter how badly I need this to work out for my own peace of mind."

"I want to honor Granny Frances's memory. And if this is what she wants—" He left the rest of his sentence unspoken. His voice was strong and even—everything Angelica wasn't feeling.

She blew out an audible breath. "I know you don't want me to be here. I'm not exactly sure why I came back. Only that I'm here for now."

"You quit your job?"

Her lips quirked. "That's one way of putting it. My boss practically shoved me out the door. Apparently, I was more expendable than I'd believed." She chuckled at her own joke, but there wasn't much mirth to it. "So now it's Granny's ranch or nothing, at least until I can make other arrangements. In the meantime, I feel obligated to try to meet Granny's last wishes as best I can and keep this ranch in working order. For you, or whatever," she finished with a vague gesture of her hand.

His blue eyes met hers and their gazes locked. For a moment, the only thing between them was their breaths, slow, deep and steady, until they were unconsciously breathing in unison.

Her throat closed, choking off her air, and she looked away.

"Okay," he said, his voice low and gruff.

"Okay?"

"We don't have to like it, but I don't see any way around it. Without my help, Granny's ranch will crash and burn and that would be a real shame—especially since I eventually intend to claim the land. I'll consider my work on this property as my investment."

Angelica bristled, although she couldn't imagine why she would have such an odd reaction to his words.

They'd already talked about this. She'd practically promised to sell Granny's ranch to him. Maybe a little later than Rowdy had originally imagined the transaction would take place, but it *would* take place.

Eventually.

That was what they both wanted, wasn't it?

Rowdy stood and excused himself, saying he needed to finish the chores and get back to his own place. Angelica was all too happy to let him leave.

Her head was spinning and her heart was pounding.

Now that she was here, with no job and nowhere else to be, all she had was the land under her feet. With Toby totally reliant on her to take care of him, it frightened her to feel so helpless.

Maybe the reason she'd failed in Denver was she'd lacked vision and resources. She'd never cared much about money except as a way to make ends meet, at least until she got pregnant with Toby. Then she had another life to care for, and he became all that mattered.

She needed to make a new plan for what she and Toby were going to do long term. She had no solid ideas at the moment, but she'd been tossing around a few thoughts—attending a culinary arts school or cosmetology college or something, just to get her out of waiting tables.

Maybe get an associate's degree in accounting, something recession-proof that would make a decent salary for her and Toby to live on.

This way, that way and the other.

Yeah. She had no clue.

She had enough money to live on right now with what Granny had given her, and if she sold the land to Rowdy, she would have new opportunities for the first time in her adult life. She was overwhelmed considering where to go with those choices.

The only plus she could see to all this was that Rowdy would end up with Granny's land. He would do right by it, and by Granny. That was one less thing she had to worry about.

There was another thought poking out from the back of her mind, demanding attention, but it was hardly worth considering. If by some wonder she could pick up sheep farming and take after Granny, the only woman in her life she had looked up to and who had always believed in her, she would be able to provide Toby with a good, stable life.

Country life, granted, but then, had she really done well in the city?

There were a lot of hurdles in her path, to be sure, not the least of which was her bad reputation in a town that had a long memory. Even with the first baby steps in the way the church ladies had reached out to her, it wouldn't be easy to prove to anyone that she had changed, that she was a Christian now and God had made her heart new.

And Rowdy living next door? Could she ever get over the angst she felt every time she thought about him, much less saw him or spoke to him?

Was this what Granny was thinking when she wrote the notes? To make Angelica and Rowdy work together until they could get over themselves?

Confusion washed through her.

Too many questions.

Too many decisions to make.

It had appeared so cut-and-dried when she'd first come back to Serendipity, ready and willing to sell the ranch.

But now?

Who knew?

Maybe only God. This was new to her, living by faith, but she was determined to do her best to follow Him. She could only pray she would figure out what He had in mind for her and, for once, do the right thing.

The next afternoon, Rowdy met Ange to walk around Granny Frances's ranch and explain what went where and all the daily chores for which she'd be responsible.

"Ready to go?" he asked.

She slipped Toby into a sling and grabbed a notebook and pen with which, she explained, she intended to take copious notes.

"As if sheep farming can be boiled down to a list of things to do," she muttered.

Rowdy laughed and nodded in agreement. "It's more like a list of lists that never ends and rolls around in cycles from day to day."

"I'd like to see Patchwork," she said, a tingle of excitement in her tone.

Ange had spent the last eight years in the city, and even as a child living in Serendipity she'd been a preacher's kid, not a rancher's child. She hadn't learned how to ride a horse until she was a teenager, whereas he had been propped in a saddle before he could walk.

He remembered how excited she'd been the first time

he'd helped her onto the saddle, so giddy that even the docile mare had picked up on her exhilaration.

Patchwork neighed and tossed her head in greeting when they entered the barn.

"I wish I could ride her," she whispered. Her gaze twinkled and took on a starry-eyed look.

His breath caught. She had always been a dreamer. It was one of the things that had first attracted him to her.

"Well, why don't you? It will give you two the opportunity to get reacquainted and she could use the exercise."

She glanced down at Toby and her expression instantly went from animated to sober.

"Maybe someday. Right now, I have Toby. Horseback riding isn't in my near future."

He almost offered to care for Toby so she could take Patchwork out. Riding always relaxed him, and she certainly looked like she needed a break.

But he knew nothing about babies and wasn't quite comfortable taking on that kind of responsibility, even if it was only for an hour.

If Toby was his baby, everything would be different. But he wasn't.

His gut churning, Rowdy suggested they finish the tour of the property.

"The hay is over here," he said, pointing to a corner of the barn. "Granny Frances grew hay on a rotating basis every year, but she didn't need much, so she'd sell the rest off, or give it away to ranchers in need."

Ange smiled softly. "That sounds like Granny."

"The rest of the fields are composed of grass, clover and forbs, all perennials. It's important to move the sheep around so the fields don't get overgrazed."

She scribbled frantically in her notebook.

He showed her the chicken coop, but given the way her brow was scrunched, displaying both her concentration and her anxiety, he gave her a pass and told her he would teach her how to care for the chickens another time.

Rowdy sensed that Ange was feeling overwhelmed by it all. Even though he hadn't seen her for eight years and he'd never been great with reading people to begin with, he could tell from her expression how inundated she was feeling.

And who could blame her?

Any sane person would be feeling that way. He'd grown up on his sheep farm and there were still days where there was more to do than there was sunlight to do it in.

Not one thing about this situation was second nature to her, as it was to him.

If he was being sensible about it, he wouldn't care how she felt about ranch living. His heart tugged to see her so overwhelmed and confused, but his head reminded him otherwise and he was the one most conflicted by it all.

Ange was dangerous.

Off-limits.

But the fact that her floundering was to his advantage didn't play well with him. No matter what their past, Ange was going through some major life changes right now, and he couldn't help but want to cut her a break.

More the fool, him.

Throughout the visit to the barn, Angelica had tented a pastel green receiving blanket over her shoulder and the fabric sling in order to protect Toby from the dust hanging in the air in the stable and then again when the sun shone too brightly on his chubby face. When clouds covered the direct sunlight, Ange uncovered him and let him enjoy the fresh country air. He was the cutest little thing, making the occasional mewling coo, sucking noisily on his fist and appearing quite content just riding along with his mama.

"I tried a pacifier but he always preferred his thumb," Ange said with a chuckle.

For reasons unknown to Rowdy, the baby sounds choked him up. He couldn't even put names to the emotions he was feeling—or why he was feeling anything at all.

It wasn't like Toby was *his* baby.

But he could have been.

If Ange hadn't freaked out and bolted before their wedding.

There it was.

The real reason the infant was getting to him. Not that he was cute or cuddly, although he was both.

But because he wasn't Rowdy's.

He tightened the reins on his emotions and focused on the tour he was giving.

Toby slept through most of the walk around the ranch, making the proverb "sleeping like a baby" come to life right before Rowdy's eyes. He had never seen such a peaceful sight as Toby curled onto Angelica's shoulder. Not even a newborn lamb could compare.

Several times the notion that they could have been a family sneaked up on him. And every time it treaded by, it sucker punched him.

Time and again he fought it as all the air left his

lungs in a whoosh, recovering as quickly as he could and pushing his emotions back into the recesses of his heart before Ange could read them on his face.

She'd always been good at knowing what he was thinking, guessing how he felt, and that was the last thing he wanted to have happen now.

There had been a time in his life when that trait had reassured him, but not anymore. They were way, *way* past that point in their lives.

He'd moved on.

Kind of.

He had buried what had happened with Angelica just as deep as it could go. He lived alone, but he wasn't lonely most of the time.

So why was he experiencing this sudden sense of panic in her presence?

The answer was obvious.

He'd come to grips with his past, and now he was inviting that very same past into his present situation, rather like aiming a runaway train toward a caved-in bridge and giving it the go-ahead to move forward.

This was crazy.

He was crazy.

But he had to believe it wouldn't always be like this, the way he experienced a twinge in his heart every time he so much as thought of Ange.

Otherwise, he wouldn't be able to function. And he couldn't run a ranch—*two* ranches—without giving it his full mental and physical effort.

The ache would ease eventually, wouldn't it?

He returned his mind to the task at hand with some difficulty. He had moved the flock of sheep—the very subject of Granny's last letter—to the closest field, so they could walk to it. Walking wasn't quite as effortless as he'd let on, but he never let his injury stop him. He wasn't about to let it interfere with his work, so he sucked it up and used a walking stick to help him balance with his bad leg.

"Ready to go?" he asked.

Ange's gaze widened. "There's more?"

He grinned. "I've saved the best for last."

He whistled for the border collies to accompany him and had them move the sheep forward so he didn't have as far to go.

As the dogs brought the flock to them, nipping on their heels to keep them moving in the right direction, Rowdy turned his attention to Toby.

"He sleeps a lot, doesn't he?" Rowdy asked, keeping his voice low, so as not to disturb the infant's rest. "Or is he one of those babies who have their nights and days mixed up?"

"Toby is the perfect baby," Ange acknowledged, smiling softly at her son. "He does sleep a lot, day and night. More than most babies, I imagine, but he's very responsive when he's awake and rarely fusses at all."

An awkward silence stretched between them, a chasm Rowdy didn't know how to breach or even if he wanted to try.

"What about Toby's father?" he asked. It was none of his business, but he couldn't contain his curiosity. "Is he in the picture?"

Her face turned bright pink, her expression an alarming combination of embarrassment and anger.

"No. Josh is *not* in the picture. I dated him for two years, and I thought our relationship was serious. And I was very foolish with how I conducted myself during that time. He spent more time at my apartment than his own, but we never talked about marriage. That is, until…"

Her words dropped off and she shook her head.

What had she been about to say?

Until she discovered she was pregnant?

Had Josh reevaluated his life and wanted to marry her then? Be a good father to Toby, even if he hadn't been a good man to Ange?

Rowdy had zero respect for a man who didn't put a ring on the finger of the woman he loved. Shacking up with a woman was the coward's way out.

Even though in Rowdy's own case his relationship with Ange had turned out in heartbreak, he had been ready to fully commit to her, to give her all of his future, his protection, his heart and his life.

"I was incredibly stupid and completely blind where Josh was concerned. I don't know what I was thinking." She sighed. "Yes, I do. I wasn't thinking at all. I met him when I was serving at a corporate function. He was a big shot with lots of money and little small-town me fell for his outward charm and charisma. Even when I realized he wasn't the person I thought him to be, I didn't walk away. I kept waiting and hoping things would get better between us. I learned the hard way that a woman can't change a man's character.

"But it wasn't only that. I wasn't looking in the right place to find peace and acceptance.

"My whole world changed the moment I found out I was pregnant with Toby. For the first time, I genuinely sought God and found forgiveness. The Lord changed my heart and my life.

"But my change of heart didn't change my circumstances. That was all on me and my foolish choices. So now, it's up to me to dig my way out of them and make something of myself, somebody Toby can be proud of."

Rowdy had always known Ange to be a determined woman, but he'd never seen a spark of dedication like the one she now carried in her beautiful blue eyes.

Had her relationship with the Lord really changed her heart and life that much? Her words sounded so genuine. He wanted to believe them. He wanted to believe *her*.

But Rowdy didn't know if he could trust her, and he definitely couldn't trust his heart to figure out what was really happening with Ange.

"Am I ashamed of the way Toby was conceived out of wedlock?" she continued, even though that question wouldn't have been something Rowdy would ever have asked. She didn't quite meet his eyes until she answered her own question.

"Yes," she affirmed. "I'm terribly humiliated every time I think about that part of my life. But keeping my sweet baby? There was never even the smallest hesitation in my mind and heart. Not for one second. Like I said before, Toby is the biggest blessing in my life."

"Surely Toby's father is obligated to pay child support, at least? Even if he doesn't want to be part of Toby's life?"

Rowdy couldn't imagine a man who would abandon his wife—*girlfriend*, he mentally amended—and their child when Ange and Toby needed him most.

It hadn't taken him long to form an opinion about this Josh fellow, and it wasn't a good one.

She scoffed. "Obligated? Perhaps. But it's not something I intend to pursue. Josh adamantly refused to acknowledge that Toby was his child from the get-go.

When I told him I was pregnant, he called me a host of bad names I don't care to repeat and insisted Toby wasn't his, even though he knew full well he was the only man I had ever been with.

"And then he walked away. I don't know where Josh is, and I don't want to know. But he was absolutely right about one thing. He is *not* Toby's father. Not in any of the ways that matter. It takes more than biology to make a dad."

Rowdy growled, agreeing wholeheartedly with Ange's statement. This Josh guy wasn't good enough for Ange and Toby, and leaving was probably the best thing that he could have done for them.

It sounded as if she would have been miserable living with the dishonorable jerk. And good riddance to him. But Rowdy still thought Josh should be throttled for walking away from his responsibilities.

"I know in the best of all worlds Toby would be raised by both a loving mother *and* father. I wish it was that cut-and-dried, but that simply isn't our reality.

"Toby and I will be okay. I'll do whatever I have to do to raise my baby on my own. I'm not the first woman who has ever found herself a single parent, and I won't be the last. But I'm bound and determined to be the very best mother I can be."

"I believe you," he said, his throat tightening around his words and making them come out in a deep baritone.

Her surprised gaze swept to his, but he didn't want to explain his last statement.

It wasn't admiration. It was a point of fact.

Ange had proven herself resilient.

And she continued to do so. Perhaps Granny Frances had wanted her to test her mettle on the ranch. To remind Ange how strong she was, that she could do more than just survive.

Rowdy felt like he was starting to get it now, to understand Granny Frances's motivations.

That was all well and good. Living a ranching lifestyle for a while would be good for her. He only hoped Granny Frances's little experiment didn't go *too* well. The last thing he wanted was Ange as a permanent next-door neighbor.

What he wanted—*needed*—was her land.

That was the end game.

It occurred to him that he *could* walk away.

Right here.

Right now.

And leave her flailing.

Failing.

Watch her fall.

But Rowdy wasn't that man.

Maybe Granny Frances wasn't just testing Ange. Perhaps the letter was to prove Rowdy's mettle, as well.

He already knew who he was—a man of the land, proud of the work he did. A man of strength and integrity, who helped the frail and the weak, and offered an arm to anyone who needed a hand up.

And at this moment, the person in need of a hand up was Ange.

He stopped at the gate that led to the pasture the sheep were grazing in and turned to Ange, crossing his arms and leaning a hip on the wooden gatepost.

Her gaze spanned the flock and then she wrinkled her nose as the scent of sheep assaulted her nostrils.

He chuckled. The sounds and smells of the ranch were like background noise to him. He didn't even notice them anymore, except for the way they soothed his heart whenever he was working with the animals.

"Well, there you have it." He gestured to the sheep, lazily grazing on the meadow grass.

Her brow furrowed and she shook her head.

"Have what? All I see are sheep."

"Exactly." He nodded, and he couldn't resist the grin that inched up one side of his lips. "Granny Frances's letter, remember."

"Yes. And?"

He made a sweeping gesture.

"Here you go. *Feed My Sheep.*"

Chapter Four

Now that she'd been introduced to some of what running a sheep farm entailed, she knew Rowdy was taking it easy on her, covering most of the ranch chores while she dealt with not one, but two major learning curves—one with the ranch and one with Toby.

Surprisingly, while sheep farming was continuing to improve at a snail's pace for her, she was doing well with Toby. As a single mother, everything fell on her shoulders—the feeding, diaper changing, washing the gazillion clothes that one baby seemed to go through. But she didn't mind a bit. Every part of caring for Toby gave her great joy.

Mothering came naturally to her, much more than she'd expected. The love that flooded through her every time she held Toby, rocked him, changed him or bent over the edge of the crib watching him peacefully sleep was immeasurable.

Even though she was perpetually fatigued by all of the recent events and upcoming decisions, she still enjoyed Toby's 2 a.m. feedings and wouldn't have it any other way. It was their personal quiet time together, where Toby nursed and Angelica prayed in the darkness.

"Are you ready to go, little man?" she murmured as she tucked Toby into his infant car seat. She'd found that was the easiest and most comfortable way to tote him around and keep him by her side while she did chores, at least for now. Plus, she could drape a light blanket over the handle to shade Toby from the sun and dust.

"What am I going to do when you grow out of your car seat?" she asked him, laughing when he gurgled back at her. "I suppose I'll deal with that problem when I come to it. Your great-granny had always said, *Let the future take care of itself. The Good Book says we've got enough to deal with right now without borrowing a cup of trouble from tomorrow.* She was a wise woman. I wish you could have met her."

She sighed. At the moment, she had more than her fair share of weighty issues that fell directly into the scope of today's problems.

She was more exhausted than she'd ever felt in her whole life. Every joint and muscle in her body ached and complained with even the smallest of movements.

How had Granny run this ranch all by herself in the twenty years since Gramps had died?

She'd never uttered one word of complaint that Angelica could remember. She'd always been cheerful and upbeat, quick with a quote from the Good Book and always ready to help a neighbor in need.

Maybe, as with Angelica, she'd saved her tears for the middle of the night.

Angelica wondered how she'd maintained her positive attitude, even when the going got tough. She'd always encouraged Angelica to look on the bright side.

There's a silver lining to every trial the Lord sees fit to walk us through, Angelica remembered Granny saying. *It's all for your own good. Every last bit.*

But back then, Angelica hadn't believed God existed. How could she, when bad things like Rowdy's rodeo accident could happen to the best, most faithful man she knew?

She knew the answer to that question. God wasn't responsible for what had happened.

She was.

She'd been the one to pressure Rowdy into riding in the saddle bronc event, something he wasn't skilled in. And all because of her ego, wanting to be able to brag on her fiancé for winning the title at the ranch rodeo.

"We've got a trial today, Toby," she told her son as she picked him up and slid the car seat into the crook of her elbow. "I'm guessing this new day will be loaded with challenges. I wish I could share a quote from the Good Book the way Granny used to do. But I'll get there, buddy. I'll get there. For now, let's go find Rowdy."

She knew he would be somewhere around the Carmichael ranch. He always did the Bar C chores in the late afternoons after the work on his own ranch was finished.

Yesterday, he'd reintroduced her to Granny's pinto quarter horse mare Patchwork. So far, Angelica didn't know or genuinely care much about ranch life, but she did like horses and was excited for the opportunity to eventually take a ride on Patchwork.

"I spent a lot of time here when I was in high school," she told Toby. He stared up at her with his wide blue eyes, as if he understood every word she was saying.

"Your grandpa and grandma were very strict and didn't allow me to date. Rowdy and I had to meet on the sly. Fortunately for us, Granny was a romantic at heart. She understood our secret love for each other and we ended up spending much of our time here at Granny's ranch.

"Sometimes Rowdy would bring over his gelding and Granny would let me borrow one of her horses to go riding with. They were some of my favorite times."

Memories rushed back, but for once they weren't all cloudy and painful. Rowdy had taught her how to ride, how to tack up her horse and how to care for it—everything from brushing and feeding to mucking out the stalls.

Everything had seemed such a sheer joy when she was with Rowdy. He made everything in her life better and more bearable, even when her home life wasn't the best.

Until she'd ruined everything.

And now she felt like she had a second chance. Not for a relationship with Rowdy. That was far too much for her to even consider. She'd burned those bridges. But one day perhaps they could at least be friends.

She found Rowdy carrying a bag of chicken feed slung over one shoulder and a bag of scratch grains on the other, walking from the barn to the coop. The sacks had to be heavy. Angelica judged them to be about fifty pounds each, but he toted them around as if they weighed nothing. The only signs of strain were the bulges in his biceps and the telltale ripples of his chest muscles when he tossed the bag down just outside the chicken coop.

Angelica averted her eyes for a moment and took a

deep breath. It would not do to have Rowdy look up and see her gaping at him in appreciation.

And she did appreciate, however covertly.

Could she help it if he was drop-dead gorgeous?

"How's Toby?" he asked, lifting his black cowboy hat by the crown and dabbing his forehead with his shirtsleeve.

"He's fine," she said, stifling a yawn. "He decided he wanted an extra meal last night, though, so he should sleep well while we cover today's chores."

"Hmm. Good."

But I'm thoroughly exhausted, thank you for asking.

Which, of course, he didn't.

Why would he?

So she didn't share her snark out loud.

The truth was, Rowdy had barely acknowledged her at all since he'd walked up. Instead, his attention was entirely focused on the baby.

She set the car seat down near enough to the chicken coop for her to be able to see and hear Toby if he cried out to her, but not close enough for him to inhale any dust or ick scratched up by the chickens.

Rowdy crouched before the baby, making high, nonsense noises and wiggling his fingers until Toby caught his thumb.

Rowdy grinned. "He's got a good grip, this one. I'll bet he'll grow up to be a real bruiser."

Angelica's heart warmed. After the wringer she'd been put through with Josh, she appreciated Rowdy's attentiveness to Toby.

She only hoped that someday Toby would have as good a male role model as Rowdy would be. She couldn't think of anyone who would be better at coaching her son into honorable manhood and showing him the things he needed to know to be successful in life.

But there was no point in going down that road, even if it was just in her mind.

She didn't know if she belonged in Serendipity, where her reputation was shredded, possibly beyond repair. She might not care for city living, either, but at least Toby would have all the advantages life in the city had to offer—the special schools where he could meet kids just like him. Education. Sports. The arts.

She had to keep her head on straight and realize there was an end to the path she was on right now. She and Toby would no doubt be out of here the moment she was certain she'd fulfilled Granny's last wish.

Although come to think of it, how would she know when she had received the last envelope?

She supposed she'd have to rely on Jo to guide her, and hope the woman didn't have any ulterior plans that would hold her up from moving on with her life.

Whatever that life was going to look like. She continued to think about it, and she still didn't know.

But in the meantime, she would do her best to work hard at Granny's ranch as Granny had apparently wanted her to do. Feed her sheep and take care of the rest of her animals.

"He's sleeping," Rowdy whispered, a rasp scraping against his usual smooth baritone. He carefully removed his thumb from Toby's grasp and covered the seat with a thin blue receiving blanket.

Stretching to his full height, he turned to Angelica. "I guess we need to get to work."

She stifled another yawn against the back of her hand.

"Chickens are on the docket for today, aren't they?" she asked hesitantly.

Angelica didn't know whether it was the muted tone of her voice or her anxious expression, but Rowdy narrowed his gaze on her.

Was that concern she saw in his eyes?

"Are you sure you're up to this?" he asked bluntly, though with enough genuine concern that the question didn't come out bristly. "You look like you're going to fall asleep standing up. Maybe we should save this for another day."

She gestured his query away. "I'm a little tired is all. Nothing I can't overcome with a little determination."

"You always were strong willed."

Angelica couldn't tell by his expression or the tone of his voice whether or not he was complimenting her, so she let the comment go.

"I thought I'd introduce you to Granny Frances's hens today." He nodded toward the chicken coop. "Thanks to them, you'll always have plenty of fresh eggs to cook with."

Angelica's gut tightened.

She liked eggs.

Scrambled eggs was one of the few dishes she could cook on her own.

What she didn't like was how she would have to get the eggs. She wasn't a big fan of chickens—or of any type of bird, really. The truth was, with all of their flapping and clawing and clucking, hens frightened her.

She was terrified that if one of them flapped up at her or got next to her face, she was going to make a total fool of herself.

She'd seen one brightly colored rooster roaming

around on the lawn outside the coop, and up until now, she'd managed to avoid it completely. She'd meant to ask Rowdy why that chicken moved about freely while the other chickens were confined, but she supposed she'd probably get the answer to that question today.

She'd been happy to studiously avoid both the brightly colored chicken *and* the rest of them in the coop, but now all that was about to end.

As Rowdy had said, she was strong willed. She could overcome her fear of chickens. She just had to face it down and work through it.

Maybe the best way to power through her phobia would be to stand right in the middle of the coop until she felt comfortable.

Or she keeled over.

Holding her breath.

With her eyes closed.

Her heart hammered but she forced herself to breathe. Rowdy would be right beside her and he would notice if she started acting funny.

Anyway, how bad could it be?

"Ready?" Rowdy unfolded a knife from his pocket and ripped into the feed, then plunged a scooper into the grain and filled a nearby blue bucket with it.

"Here you go," he told her, passing the bucket to her and flashing an encouraging grin.

"What am I supposed to do with this?"

Rowdy pointed to a feeder box and watering tin cleverly using the space under the henhouse. "Food. Water. Right under the henhouse where they roost and sleep. And this," he said, pointing around the fenced enclosure, "is called the run."

"And we go in and shut the gate behind us?"

She already knew the answer to her question, but she was quite literally shaking in her mud boots. She supposed she'd hoped he'd take pity on her and show her how to do it without her actually having to set foot in the coop herself.

If wishes were horses…

Or anything but chickens.

"I know Granny Frances said we were supposed to feed the sheep, and that's a good start for you, but the chickens are by default part of the package while you're living here at the ranch."

"Unfortunately," she mumbled under her breath.

"What was that?" His brow rose in time with one side of his lips.

She didn't answer him, but instead, opened the gate to the chicken run and stepped through, not even looking to see if Rowdy followed.

Either way, this was on her.

I can do this, she told herself.

I can do this with God's help, she mentally amended.

Her adrenaline spiked when she heard the clang of the gate closing behind her.

A few hens in various shades of brown milled around, scratching and pecking at the fresh pine shavings that covered the ground.

"We have to change the pine shavings frequently to keep the run clean, but let's not worry about it today. I usually spread some scratch grain on the ground in the run. It gives the hens something interesting to do. That's what they're looking for."

A few chickens showed a mild interest in Angelica— or rather her feed bucket—but none of them charged at her with wings flapping and beaks pecking as she'd feared they might do.

See?

She was being irrational.

Fear conquered.

"Dump the feed, and afterward we can grab the hose and fill the water bin."

While she followed Rowdy's instructions, he spread the scratch grain across the run and the hens immediately turned to their dinner.

"Next, we find the eggs," Rowdy said.

Angelica froze right where she was. Were there eggs hidden under the pine shavings somewhere? Would her next step crush a fresh egg and then she'd be on cleaning duty?

"What, like an Easter egg hunt or something?" She tried to sound casual, but her laugh sounded as if she was choking on something.

Rowdy snorted. "It's not quite as complicated as all that. While there are occasions where a hen drops an egg in an odd place, it's a pretty good bet that we'll find most of them in the henhouse where they roost."

"Oh." Heat rose to her cheeks. Every time she opened her mouth, she sounded more and more like the uneducated not-a-rancher that she was.

"It's pretty simple, really," Rowdy said, appearing not to notice how flushed her face must look. "You just check all the nests. If a chicken is roosting and doesn't feel like wandering out into the pen, you check underneath her, grab the egg and put it in the bucket."

Angelica watched while he demonstrated, jamming his hand under the nearest roosting hen, causing her to flap her wings and cluck in complaint.

But despite the chicken's fuss, Rowdy came up with a light brown egg, which he brandished in triumph before placing it into the bucket.

"This part, at least, is a little bit like having an Easter egg hunt." He grinned at her. "Easy as pie. Have at it."

She shook her head and crossed her arms.

"What's wrong?"

"There is no possible way you are going to get me to stick my hand under—" she gestured toward the chicken he'd just taken the egg from "—that." Her voice was no more than a croak.

He bent his head toward her, an amused half smile on his lips.

"What's the problem?"

She opened her mouth to speak but no words came forth. How could she explain herself without confiding in him, displaying her vulnerability and embarrassment, neither being emotions she wished to share with Rowdy.

"I don't like…birds." She took a quick gulp of air. "Actually, I have an irrational fear of them," she finally admitted.

"Really?" he asked, surprised. "Did you watch one too many horror movies when you were a kid?"

She snorted and shook her head. If only it was that easy.

"If you must know, I was out camping with some friends last year and a swarm of hummingbirds decided to dive-bomb me. I am *so* not joking. The buzz of their wings and—ugh!"

She swiped in front of her face as if the hummingbirds were still there.

Rowdy's lips twitched and she narrowed her eyes on

him. He gave a valiant effort, but eventually he threw back his head and laughed at the picture she'd painted.

"Excuse me," she protested. "I'm serious here. I ran back to the RV and didn't emerge again until nightfall, when the idea of s'mores finally tempted me back out near the campfire."

"There's quite a difference between hummingbirds and chickens."

She rolled her eyes. "Thank you for pointing that out, Captain Obvious. Now tell me something I don't know."

"Chickens are awesome?" he tried, a chuckle following his words.

"No, I don't think so. Try again."

"I think, given this new morsel of information, that I went about today's lesson all wrong. I didn't realize there might be—*issues*—where chickens were concerned."

"Oh, cut it out. I can't possibly be the only one who doesn't like chickens. You don't have problems because you grew up on a ranch. This is all second nature to you. For me, not so much."

"Right." He stroked his stubbled jaw and scanned the chicken run, as if he was looking for something.

"Ah. Here we go," he said, scooping a chicken into his hands and tucking it under his arm, holding it like a running back would hold a football.

"This here is Lucy," he said in the soft Texas drawl that had always melted Angelica's heart. She'd lost much of her own accent after living in Denver for as long as she had.

"What are we going to do with—er—Lucy?" she asked tentatively.

"Just pet her a bit. Get used to her. Don't worry. I've got a good hold on her."

"She won't peck me?"

He chuckled. "No. Lucy is perfectly tame."

"So I just um, pet her like a dog?"

"Mostly, except she has feathers and not fur. Lucy doesn't mind the attention, do you, Luc?"

The chicken didn't so much as cluck, which Angelica took as an affirmative answer, so, holding her breath, she ran her hand along the bird's feathers, which were surprisingly soft.

"How about that?" she murmured. "Are all the hens as mellow as Lucy?"

"For the most part. Once in a while, you'll get one in a dither about something. That's when they'll peck at you a bit. Just show them who's boss. They're really nothing to be afraid of," he added with a grin.

"Says you. Great. Thanks for the encouragement," she said drily.

"Any time."

He passed Lucy to Angelica and showed her how to hold the chicken. For a full minute, she stood as still as a board, afraid to move, with Lucy under her arm.

But she was holding a *chicken*.

That was progress.

Conquer the fear, she coaxed herself. *Embrace it, and then move beyond it.*

Swallowing hard, she set Lucy on the ground and picked up another hen, just as she'd seen Rowdy do.

The second chicken wasn't quite as docile as Lucy had been, but she didn't try to bite. Angelica called that a win.

Setting the second hen down, she made a tour of the

run, determined to touch every last chicken and face down her phobia, send her fears flying—no pun intended—hopefully never to return.

She even slid her hand underneath a roosting hen in the henhouse, exclaiming in delight when she withdrew a bluish-green egg.

Easter eggs, indeed.

A couple of the hens balked, clucking and flapping away from her at her sudden triumphant cheer, but she barely noticed. She had an egg in her hand.

Yessss!

Fist pump.

"You got it, girl," Rowdy praised.

Angelica grinned as her heartbeat slowed. One of her daily chores would be caring for these chickens and gathering eggs.

And she could do it.

She might even learn all their names.

She'd still have to continue fighting her phobia. As much as she would like for it to, it wouldn't go away in one fell swoop, but every time she conquered her fear and entered the chicken run it would become less and less of an issue until eventually she wouldn't think about it at all.

Setting the egg in the bucket Rowdy held out to her, she brushed her palms across her blue jeans and headed back through the coop's metal gate.

Toby picked that moment to make his presence known. He was awake and crying softly, the sweet *ah-wah, ah-wah* of an infant.

"We'd better go in and wash up before I pick up Toby with these grimy hands."

"Mind if I join you?" Rowdy asked. "I'd like to hold the little guy for a minute, if that's okay with you."

Angelica's heart flipped in response. Not too many guys would want to hold a baby who wasn't their own flesh and blood, especially one with special needs.

But Rowdy wasn't most guys.

It wasn't that Rowdy was treating Toby special because he had special needs. Rather, it was more like he just accepted Toby the way the Lord had made him with all of the dignity and respect he deserved as one of God's children.

She reached for the car seat but Rowdy beat her to it. "I'll get him."

Angelica didn't argue. Her arms perpetually ached from lugging the car seat around with her everywhere, although she would suffer no end to aches and pains for the sake of her precious son.

As the three of them walked back toward the house, Angelica spotted, out of the corner of her eye, the multicolored rooster running loose across the yard.

She wondered why the rooster was so brightly colored in hues of blues, greens, reds and golds, while its fellow chickens were all feathered in shades of drabby browns and tans. And she'd forgotten to ask why the rooster ran loose when the others were cooped up.

She'd touched every chicken on the property except this one. If she was going to face down her fears, she might as well be off and running at a one hundred percent success rate.

Without informing Rowdy of her intentions, she turned and strode straight toward the rooster. She half expected it to flap away to freedom since it wasn't cooped up, but instead, this one appeared to be preparing to face her down.

A chill of alarm zipped down her spine as the chicken puffed itself up and raised its wingspan in an attempt to make itself look bigger.

It looked big enough even without the aggressive movements, and plenty scary when it squawked a warning to her.

It's just a chicken, she reminded herself. It was probably acting that way because she'd startled it and caught it off-guard.

No matter.

She was bigger than this rooster and stronger than her fear.

Taking a deep breath for courage, she stalked forward and held out her hand, determined to touch the colorful rooster's back and end her day on a win.

It was only after she'd firmly committed herself and was mere inches away from the chicken that Rowdy's frantic shout cut through the pounding adrenaline.

"No, Ange. Wait! Don't!"

Rowdy had been deep in thought, wrestling with his stray feelings for Ange and Toby, when suddenly Ange had vectored off the path.

At first, he didn't comprehend her direction or realize where she was heading—that is, until the bantam rooster in the yard squawked and ruffled his feathers.

Rowdy's adrenaline spiked and every nerve ending leapt to life.

What did Ange think she was doing?

Facing down her fear, he realized, too little, too late. Just as she had done in the henhouse.

To her inexperienced eye, a chicken was a chicken was a chicken.

This was *so* not going to end well.

As quickly and gently as possible, Rowdy set down the car seat and lunged for Ange.

Her hand was already well within the rooster's strike zone.

"Ouch," she screeched as she snapped her hand back from the angry rooster. She shook out her fingers. "Ow, ow, ow! It bit me. Twice."

"You need to—" Rowdy started, but Ange was already following the instructions he had yet to give.

She twisted away from the ticked-off rooster and bolted the other direction—also, Rowdy noted, well away from where Rowdy had set Toby. Even in her own distress, her first priority was on protecting her baby.

"Help," she called, zigzagging around and looking behind her, only to realize the rooster was gaining on her. Its wingspan and clucking would be intimidating to even the heartiest of country folk, and Ange was afraid of birds to begin with.

The bantam pecked at her jeans-clad legs repeatedly. Rowdy had been around roosters enough to know this encounter would leave bruises.

But the real damage would be internal.

This was Ange's worst nightmare come to life, especially when the rooster started flapping his wings up toward her face.

With the full-on rooster deluge, Ange wasn't watching where she was going and her feet hit on a patch of loose gravel.

Before Rowdy could so much as lunge in her direction, she'd fallen hard onto the earth, tucking her knees into her chest and protecting her head with her arms.

"Rowdy," she screamed.

His heart was beating out of his chest by the time he reached her.

With one well-timed leap, he batted the rooster away with the palm of his hand and then took his place between Ange and Psycho Rooster to carry on the battle.

Taking the rooster's lead, Rowdy drew himself up to his full height, straightening his shoulders and holding his arms out full-length, palms facing outward, making himself look as large and intimidating as possible.

When the rooster squawked at him, he shouted back.

"Shoo. Get out of here."

Still, the rooster attacked, flying at Rowdy's face, his pointed claws extended.

Rowdy grabbed the rooster's legs and then tucked him under his arm and held on tight, ignoring the pecks and scratches on his forearms and the rivulets of blood dripping from his jaw.

He marched the rooster none too gently to the back of the house and released him, pushing him away and hollering after him.

"Shoo, you naughty fellow. Get on out of here."

He followed up by chasing the rooster a few uneven steps for good measure. Rowdy's limp was always more pronounced when his dander was up, and he was good and angry now.

No agitated rooster was going to attack Ange.

Not on his watch.

His heart was thumping loudly in his chest. What if Ange had been holding Toby?

He refused to follow those thoughts to their logical conclusions. Ange and Toby would be gone soon, back to the city. He doubted she'd run into any Psycho Roosters in Denver.

After he was certain the rooster wasn't going to turn back to follow him and continue the fight, Rowdy jogged back to Ange.

She'd rolled to a sitting position, her arms wrapped protectively around her knees while she attempted to catch her breath.

"What was *that*?" she asked with a grimace.

"The meanest rooster in Texas. The only person that ornery bird ever respected was Granny Frances. What possessed you to chase him, anyway?"

Her cheeks flushed a pretty pink.

"I just wanted to touch him the way I had done with all of the other chickens, so I could call my phobia-conquering exercise a complete success. How was I supposed to know it would freak out on me?"

"Quick lesson on chickens. The nondescript brown ones are hens. That colorful guy is a rooster. He struts around with all those fancy feathers to impress the ladies. Hens are by and large friendly creatures. Roosters, not so much. Better you just stay away from that one."

Ange snorted, then stood and brushed off her jeans. "You don't have to tell me *that* twice."

She shook her head and laughed. "Well, I can definitely chalk that one up to a learning experience."

Rowdy was surprised she could laugh about it quite so easily—and so soon after the encounter.

Sure, it was the kind of story that would be passed around the family table during holidays for years to come, but right this second, Rowdy's heart was still beating half out of his chest.

Ange could have been seriously hurt.

"Rowdy," Ange said, touching his jaw and gently turning his head so she could get a better look at the left side of his face. "You're injured."

He shook his head and held his hands up, palms out. "It's nothing."

"It's not nothing. You're bleeding."

She took his hands in hers and turned them over, examining both sides of his arms.

He shrugged. Okay, so he had a few bites and scratches. He'd had worse.

"You are coming in with me," she said in an unyielding tone that reminded him of Granny. All attitude and no-nonsense. "I remember Granny kept a first-aid kit in one of the kitchen cabinets. Hopefully it's still there."

"That's really not necessary," he protested.

At that moment, Toby wailed in earnest, making his presence known as only a tiny baby can do.

"It sounds like you've got your hands full with your son," Rowdy said with a chuckle.

"Those scratches are not nothing, and I'm not taking no for an answer. It was my fault you got hurt. Again." She choked out that last word.

What did she mean, *again*?

At first, he thought she must be referring to some physical incident, but that couldn't be right.

It took him a minute to sort through his memories and realize she must be talking about emotional pain—something far more damaging than any rooster could do.

The wedding.

His heartbreak.

He definitely didn't want to go there.

"Okay. I think you're making way more of this than it is, but lead the way," he conceded, more to get out of the possibility of having to talk about what happened eight years ago than because he really needed bandaging up.

He gestured toward the house, but she didn't go on ahead of him as he'd expected her to do. Rather, she picked up Toby and placed the car seat handle in the crook of one arm and then slipped her other hand under Rowdy's elbow, as if to somehow support him as he walked.

Which was the outside of ridiculous. Yes, he walked with a limp, but he'd had to deal with that for many years since a freak accident at a ranch rodeo and it didn't slow him down much.

Granted, he was pretty scratched up by his wrestling match with Psycho Rooster, but the steady streams of blood made the injuries look much worse than they appeared. A clean scrubbing with soap and water and he would be as good as new.

Still, he humored her, understanding that she needed to feel as if she was doing something useful.

Before long, they had reached Granny Frances's ranch house. They washed their hands and Ange put Toby down for a nap. Then she seated him at the table in the kitchen and carefully peeled off his blue chambray shirt, leaving him in a white T-shirt, his arms bare.

In moments, she had his arms on the tabletop, couched in a soft towel, while she rummaged through the cupboards for the first-aid kit.

She opened the kit on the table and clicked her tongue against her teeth as she rummaged through the contents. She finally settled on several large bandages, rolls of gauze and tape and some antibiotic ointment.

He was going to be as trussed up as a Thanksgiving turkey by the time she was finished with him if she used all that stuff. His vote was still on soap and water.

But then again, if he'd been alone, he never would have been taking on a mad rooster to defend Ange.

Which, despite his injuries, felt pretty good.

The adrenaline spiking through him. The chance to be a hero. He led a secluded lifestyle on his ranch, so he would take what he could get.

Even if it was stupid.

He sucked in a breath through his teeth when she dabbed at a particularly deep scratch along his forearm with the corner of a wet washcloth.

"What is *on* that thing?"

Her gaze widened. "Rubbing alcohol, of course."

The alcohol burned through the open wound and it was all he could do not to leap off his chair.

"Hold still," she said. Her voice was gentle but she had a death grip on his wrist. "I have to make sure the wound is clean before I bandage it."

"By digging to China? Why did you have to go and use rubbing alcohol? A little soap and water would have sufficed just fine."

"You may be the expert in ranch living, but I took a course in first aid before Toby was born and I am Red Cross certified. Who knows what kind of germs those awful claws are carrying? I don't want any of your wounds to become infected. As it is, that one on your jaw may leave a scar."

A scar?

Cool.

Didn't scars make a man look rugged?

The ladies loved them, right?

Somehow, he suspected Ange wouldn't feel the same way if he were to voice his thoughts.

"That chicken really did some damage."

"Rooster," he corrected without thinking.

"Right. Rooster. The one with the bright feathers. I won't make *that* mistake again. Thankfully, they don't have roosters running loose in downtown Denver."

Rowdy assumed such a statement was meant to reassure him, and he guessed in a way it did. She and Toby would be gone before long, and the land would be his.

But there was a part of him that didn't want her to go, at least not yet. They had unfinished business. He had not yet taught her to know and love sheep farming, and maybe catch a glimpse of what might have been if she had not run off on him the night before their wedding.

Maybe—okay, *probably*—it was wrong for him to harbor those kinds of feelings, almost as if he was plotting some sort of emotional revenge on her.

But was it so wrong that he wanted to open her eyes? That he wanted her to *see*?

He watched her as she tended to his wounds, gently wiping away the blood and dabbing at the gouges. A lock of long light blond hair dropped over her shoulder and he reached out with his free hand to tuck it back behind her ear, barely resisting the urge to take an extra moment to enjoy the silky feel of her locks, to run them through his fingers to see if her hair was as soft as he remembered.

Rowdy concentrated on not moving his arms as she worked, using the sting of the rubbing alcohol to force his mind away from the road his heart wanted to travel.

The baby monitor crackled as Toby woke with a howl that brought a smile to one side of Rowdy's lips.

"That was a short nap," Ange said. "Excuse me a minute while I go grab him."

How could a baby's cry sound so bloomin' cute? That Toby was in distress in some way—hungry or wet or just needing his mama's arms—shouldn't make Rowdy smile, but something about the mewl went straight to his heart and swelled within it.

Melted it.

What was that, anyway?

Joy?

How could a little squeak from a baby that was not only not of his own blood, but was his ex-fiancée's, have any kind of hold on him whatsoever?

Danger zone.

Somehow, the pain of his past was getting muddled with the confusion of the present.

A cloud of panic overshadowed him as he mentally twisted and turned to avoid making contact with those befuddling emotions.

He had better get out now, while the going was good.

He bolted to a standing position, hitting the table with his thigh and nearly upending the first-aid kit.

"Is Toby hungry?" he asked, as if Ange hadn't noticed that the infant hadn't settled down. She'd been making soft, soothing baby talk to him from the moment he'd awoken, promising her full attention just as soon as Rowdy's injuries were taken care of.

"Sit down, Rowdy," she said, placing Toby in the bouncer. "Toby is fine. He can wait one more minute while I finish patching you up. He only sounds like he's going to perish from lack of sustenance."

"Still, I'd better go."

He grabbed his chambray shirt from the back of the chair and threaded his still-stinging arms through it.

There were a few spots where rivulets of blood still dripped from his forearms, but he ignored them.

"You're being stubborn. Not to mention you're bleeding all over your chambray. Come on. Let me help you."

Her voice was as calm and gentle as a mythical siren's song. It was all Rowdy could do not to slump back into his seat and give in to her ministrations.

But that, he knew, would be a major tactical error. His emotions were all over the place after the adrenaline rush when Ange was attacked.

Stupid rooster.

"Look. You just take care of Toby, and I'll clean myself up. See you tomorrow."

He scrambled toward freedom and was out the front door before she could open her mouth to argue.

Whew. Narrow escape.

Chapter Five

❦

Take care of Toby.

What was that supposed to mean?

She'd mulled over his words all through the night but had come up empty.

Was Rowdy judging her as a mother just because she'd been concerned about his injuries and had left Toby to his own devices for the few minutes it would have taken to patch him up?

How fair was that?

It wasn't as if Toby would have starved to death. Angelica knew her son well enough to know he would find his fist and amuse himself until she could get to him.

As she dressed, she again went over and over Rowdy's words in her mind and the strange way he'd left, saying something ridiculous about not wanting to bleed on the baby.

Wasn't the whole point that she was trying to patch him up so he wouldn't bleed on Toby, or anyone else, for that matter? And that was the thanks she got?

She yawned as she readied Toby for the day. Mornings came early on the ranch, but that was okay with

Angelica. Toby was up and at 'em the moment the sun rose, anyway.

The only conclusion she arrived at was that Rowdy was one stubborn man, leaving the house with his wounds raw and bleeding. She expected the scratch on his jaw made from that razor-sharp rooster claw would scar, especially if it wasn't taken care of immediately.

Rowdy had always been stubborn, but now he was being awfully moody, especially considering all she'd been trying to do was be nice and help him.

Well, no. That wasn't the whole truth, now, was it?

The truth was that she was trying to make amends, to make up for her past mistakes.

She snorted.

As if that could ever be done.

Rowdy was right. Those little rooster scratches, deep as they might be, were nothing in comparison to the other ways she had hurt him or that he'd been hurt on her behalf.

This latest incident proved what she'd known all along. It was the reason he had suggested they break it off all those years ago, and ultimately it was why she had left him at the altar.

She wasn't any good for Rowdy. Whenever she was near him, bad things happened to him. He was probably counting the minutes until she would be gone, so he could join Granny Frances's farm to his and live in peace.

Perhaps it was time to put a rush on this whole process. She knew in her heart of hearts that Granny was hoping for a different outcome, that Angelica and Toby would choose to make their home here, that Angelica would find the same delight Granny had working the ranch.

But that was simply not to be. While Angelica had experienced moments of joy in the past few days, her failures had far outnumbered her triumphs.

And she would not—could not—live next to Rowdy, even if acres of distance separated them.

This morning, rather than using the car seat to tote him, she slid Toby into a front pack. She needed to feel him breathing and close to her heart. Instead of his giant diaper bag, she wrapped a lunch-sack-sized bag filled with essentials over her hip.

She was as ready as she would ever be.

Rowdy had called and instructed her to leave the chickens alone for the time being, at least until he was around to guide her, which was fine by her. Phobia or no phobia, she wasn't in any hurry to step into that coop again.

Instead of feeding the chickens, she headed out to check on the sheep. Many of the late-season ewes were close to delivering, and it was her job to keep an eye out for new lambs and make sure they were all nursing properly with their mamas.

She also thought she would spend some time learning to herd the sheep with the two border collies, Kip and Tucker, and the Anatolian shepherd, Zeus, who guarded the flock at night.

At least with the dogs she could be herself, with little fear of failure. All three dogs appeared to understand that she was Granny's replacement—not that Granny could ever be replaced. But Angelica was her temporary substitute.

No doubt they'd take to Rowdy even better than they

did to her after he took over the land. It saddened her to think about what might happen to Granny's dogs once the sale of the land went through. Rowdy had been caring for the dogs in Granny's absence. Surely they had bonded. But he already had working dogs of his own. Hopefully he'd still want to keep Granny's dogs on, for her memory's sake, if for no other reason.

She remained lost in thought until she had reached the barn. She stopped and inhaled deeply. Maybe it was because she was born and raised in Serendipity and had ranching in her blood, skipping one generation notwithstanding, but it was funny how quickly she'd grown fond of the sights and sounds of the country.

Even the sweetly acrid scent of the animals, combined with the smell of fresh-cut hay and rich grain, along with leather tack, brought her mind right back to a time when Granny's house was the only fortress she had against town rumors and gossip.

It still was that stronghold. She'd found a measure of peace here that she hadn't had elsewhere.

Granny's house needed a bit of repair, and the barn needed a new coat of paint, but Rowdy could take care of those types of minor issues sometime in the future when the property officially belonged to him. Or maybe he would knock the buildings down and make more room for the sheep to graze.

Angelica moved from jug to jug in the barn, small, closed-off areas where Rowdy had sorted the ewes he believed were closest to giving birth or that he thought might have trouble with the birthing process.

She was delighted to find that two of the ewes had delivered during the night and the cute little balls of fluff were contentedly nursing with their mamas. She knew there were various inoculations to give and a few odds and ends to take care of with the new lambs, but they could wait until later this afternoon when Rowdy could attend to them. She didn't want Toby too near the ewes or the newborn lambs for health reasons.

She wasn't an expert, but both lambs looked well and she thought Rowdy would be pleased.

Next, she walked to the nearest field, where Rowdy had cut out and herded the rest of the ewes close to delivering.

She was glad for the opportunity to stretch her legs as she weaved through ankle-high grass to look for lambs that might have dropped during the night.

She didn't see anything until she reached the far end of the field in the southernmost corner, right next to the electric netting that kept the ewes safe and predators out.

Zeus was shadowing the area, barking at her as she approached.

Angelica's heartbeat soared in excitement when she saw two wobbly white newborn lambs.

Twins!

Angelica was elated at discovering the two-for-one special.

She knew Rowdy would be pleased, as well. Extra lambs meant extra money.

But as Angelica stopped to observe them for a moment, she was concerned to see that while one lamb had been warmly welcomed by its mother and was contentedly nursing, the ewe was actively butting the other little lamb away from her, denying the poor thing its right to nurse with its twin.

Did sheep sometimes reject their own young? She

suddenly wished she knew more about the animals Granny had committed to her care.

Pulse pounding, Angelica slipped her cell phone from the back pocket of her jeans and pressed Rowdy's number, which he had insisted she put on speed dial because she and Toby were living alone and he'd be the closest one to call in the case of an emergency.

Angelica wasn't certain this qualified as an emergency, but frankly, she didn't know who else to call. It was either Rowdy or the town vet, and who knew how long it would take for the vet to get here.

Plus, she knew Rowdy better, and trusted him implicitly.

"What's wrong?" Rowdy asked without so much as saying hello. "Are you okay? Is there something the matter with Toby?"

She was surprised at the depth of concern in his voice, but she quickly put him at ease on both counts.

"Toby and I are fine. But when I was walking in the field this morning looking for newborn lambs, I came upon a ewe that had just delivered twins."

"That's great," he assured her. "Ewes of this breed often have twins. It's nothing to worry about."

"Yes, well in this case, the ewe appears to be favoring one lamb over the other. She's completely rejecting one, actually, and it has me a little worried. Enough that I thought I'd better give you a call."

"You did the right thing," he said.

"Every time the second lamb moves in to try to nurse, the ewe butts it away." Her words came faster and fiercer with every syllable.

"Take a deep breath, Ange. This happens sometimes,

especially with twins. We can take care of it. Where are you right now?"

"In the southernmost corner of the lambing field. The ewe is standing just short of the fence line. You'll be able to see—and probably hear—Zeus when you get close enough. He's been hovering. He really knows his job."

"Sit tight. I have to gather a few things together and then I'll be right over."

"Okay." Relief flooded through her. She was way out of her depth here, but Rowdy would know just what to do.

Rowdy had always been that man to her, the guy she could count on, and apparently, some things hadn't changed.

She thought the words, even if they were never anything she would admit to out loud.

Hero to the rescue.

Rowdy arrived with his bucketful of equipment and quickly assessed the situation. Frankly, he was more concerned about the state he'd found Ange in than for the little lamb seemingly rejected by its mother.

She looked worried. That sensitive side of Ange's heart, her vulnerability, was something few had seen. For some reason, she kept her guard up and didn't put her emotions on display. But Rowdy knew—or he'd thought he had known—who she really was. At least, until she'd run off and abandoned him on the eve of their wedding.

But right here, right now, the soft side of her was back in spades. Her heart was breaking for the rejected twin, perhaps recognizing the parallels in her own life.

Her parents had, in all the ways that mattered to a young girl, rejected Ange when she was no more than a child.

And Toby, picking up on his mother's current distress, was squirming and wailing in the front pack, flapping his tiny arms and legs. He wasn't usually fussy, so that told Rowdy a lot.

"Finally," Ange said, laying a palm on her throat. "I feel so bad for this little lamb. How can the mother be so unfeeling to her own baby?"

"Sheep aren't the brightest animals on the planet," he explained, kneeling next to the ewe and the deserted lamb. "This ewe may not realize the second lamb is hers. She may believe she is protecting the first lamb, the one she thinks is hers, from being pushed out by the twin."

"So what do we do now?" She moved closer, but with Toby in a front pack and a diaper bag slung across her hip, there was no way for her to crouch down by the ewe.

He didn't want her getting too close to the sheep, anyway, especially since he didn't know how strong of an immune system Toby had.

But when Ange said *we*, she meant *we*. He could see it was eating her up to have to stand by and watch, unable to do anything to help.

"First, let's try to coax the ewe into feeding the lamb. Just like with a human baby, the ewe's colostrum is best for the lamb, especially for the first day."

Rowdy scooped the rejected lamb into his arm and positioned himself so his shoulder would take the brunt of the ewe's force should she balk and try to butt the lamb away again.

"You can help block the ewe's movements with your

legs, if you want, but be careful. I don't want you and Toby to get caught in the cross fire."

Rowdy half expected her to argue with him. Ange was the type of woman who always wanted to be right in the middle of the action.

But she merely nodded in agreement. "Don't worry. I'll be careful."

He tossed a glance up at her and their gazes met and held. Rowdy's throat burned and he swallowed hard.

Becoming a mother had changed Ange—in a good way. She was still the take-charge, independent woman she had always been, but somehow having Toby had softened her around the edges. He'd always known the gentle side of her was there, but she'd always chosen to hide it. Now, with Toby, that side of her personality beamed through.

The way she put Toby first in everything. That tender way she interacted with him, whether feeding him a bottle or changing a diaper.

Rowdy liked what he saw. And for the first time since she'd left him eight years ago, he allowed himself to acknowledge those feelings.

But only for a moment, since his attention needed to be completely focused on the lamb and its mama. For five minutes, Rowdy and Ange tried without success to get the rejected lamb to nurse on the ewe.

It didn't help that Toby was fussing in earnest, growing louder by the minute. Ange was desperately making shushing noises and using her hands to bounce Toby soothingly, but Toby would have none of it.

Ange flashed Rowdy an apologetic glance.

"I think he's picking up on my concern. He usually doesn't make this much noise, and it's startling the ewe."

"No worries. Why don't you go back to the house and take care of Toby and I'll keep working with the lamb? I suspect we're going to have to go with Plan B with this little girl, anyway."

"Plan B?"

"Plan Bottle-feed. I'll get it started, but I think you'll enjoy watching the process, so I'll wait for you in the barn, okay?"

Her expression shaded in disappointment. Rowdy didn't know whether she was unhappy because she had to miss watching the beginning of the process of bottle-feeding, or because they hadn't been successful in getting the lamb to suckle on its mother.

He attempted to get the lamb to nurse for an additional ten minutes, but to no avail. There was no obvious reason he could see why the ewe would reject the lamb.

It looked healthy enough to his trained eye. It was possible there was a real problem, something he couldn't see, but he wasn't going to borrow trouble. The ewe's rejection didn't necessarily mean there was anything wrong with the lamb—only that the ewe was confused.

He scooped the lamb up in one arm and lifted his bucket of supplies with the other, then trod back over the field and into the barn, whistling as he went. Working with newborn lambs was one of the real perks of ranch living, and he loved it.

He penned the lamb while he went to work giving it the necessary inoculations and cleaning it, then mixed up a bottle of sheep's colostrum.

He didn't realize Ange was back until he heard a chuckle from behind him, startling him and making his heart gallop.

"That looks familiar," Ange said. "I go through almost the exact same process when I prepare supplementary formula for Toby. Except, of course, that the lamb's bottle is much bigger."

"Yeah?" he said, testing out the temperature of the formula on the inside of his arm.

Her chuckle became a downright laugh. "I do that, too."

"Then you should be an expert at feeding. Why don't I wash up in the barn sink so I can hold Toby and let you have the honor of feeding the lamb?"

"Oh, could I?" Her eyes brightened. For someone who had no intention of sticking around and becoming a rancher, she certainly looked excited.

Then again, all babies were cute, be they humans or lambs. Maybe that was all it was.

Ange transferred Toby into Rowdy's arms and handed him a bottle of the baby's supplemental formula.

His gaze dropped to the sweet infant curled in his arms. Lambs were cute, but the little fellow blinking up at him with those big blue eyes was a whole other kind of wonderful. It got him right in the heart.

He wasn't familiar with feeding a baby, but he held Toby's bottle much as he would do with a lamb. Toby rooted for it a minute and then settled down to nurse, sucking noisily, his lips not quite sealing around the bottle. A tiny rivulet of milk dripped down his chin and Rowdy dabbed it away with the corner of the receiving blanket Toby was swaddled in.

"Same concept with the lamb," he encouraged Ange.

She awkwardly turned over the bottle, which was substantially larger than the one Rowdy was using with Toby, and pressed it to the lamb's lips.

The lamb didn't budge, as if it had no natural instinct to root for the bottle at all.

Ange sighed in frustration. "What am I doing wrong?"

"It's not you," he assured her. "She just needs a little more coaxing to be shown what to do."

Toby shifted and grunted, pushing the now-empty bottle away. The infant had certainly made quick work of *his* meal.

"Don't forget that you need to burp him," Ange reminded him. "Toby tends to swallow a lot of air when he is bottle-fed and those bubbles go deep."

Rowdy hesitated, not quite knowing what to do.

"Put him up against your shoulder and lightly pat his back," she said. "That will coax out the air."

His blank stare must have clued her in that he was walking around in entirely new territory here.

"Oh, and be sure to put a receiving blanket over your shoulder first. Those burps of his are sometimes a bit wet. You don't want to get formula all over your nice shirt."

Rowdy chuckled. He didn't care about the state of his shirt. He had a dozen just like this one, only in varying colors, hanging in his closet.

He was a cowboy. All he needed were a few T-shirts, some chambray and a couple pairs of jeans plus a Sunday service/wedding/funeral suit.

"I can't even get her to take this bottle," Ange said when the lamb continued to balk.

She shook her head and gestured toward the lamb.

"Can I give her a name?"

"A name? You mean like Rover or Charlie?" he teased. He'd always thought of his sheep by the numbers tagged in their ears. Sheep Nine or Lamb Twenty-One or something. Nothing like what Ange was suggesting.

"Well, yes, kind of," she explained. "You said this little lamb is a female, didn't you? I can't keep calling her *it* or *lamb*. It's too confusing."

Rowdy nodded, trying to conceal the smile that crept up one side of his lips as Ange's expression became thoughtful.

"How about Miss Woolsey?"

Miss Woolsey?

She had to be kidding him right now.

She wasn't kidding.

It took every ounce of his self-restraint not to break into laughter. The only thing that stopped him was how seriously Ange appeared to be taking this. She might pop him in the arm if she had any idea what was going through his mind.

Miss Woolsey.

He didn't know if she realized how difficult it was going to be to tell one lamb from another, assuming she wanted to name every one of them, which he suspected she did.

She would have to check the lamb's tag every time she wanted to address one of them by name, *and* she would have to memorize what name went with which tag. She would need a spreadsheet to keep track of it all.

He held back a snort as he imagined her carrying a physical spreadsheet around—or worse yet, an electronic tablet.

There were a lot of little lambs. He'd purposefully stretched the lambing season later for Granny Frances's flock than his own so he'd be able to work both.

"Okay. So how do I get Miss Woolsey here to nurse?"

she asked, holding up her gloved hands and the bottle the lamb was stubbornly refusing.

"Put her between your knees and coax her head up with your free hand."

He waited until Ange had maneuvered herself into position before he continued.

"Squeeze the bottle enough to get the milk flowing and wipe the contents all over her snout, especially her lips. When she latches on, stroke her neck to encourage her to swallow."

Ange did as he'd suggested and Miss Woolsey successfully connected with the bottle.

Ange gave a small whoop of joy and then shushed herself, and Rowdy chuckled in earnest. He hadn't had this much fun during lambing season in years. It was amazing what a woman's perspective—especially one who was completely unfamiliar with sheep farming—could do to a man.

"I don't want to frighten Miss Woolsey away now that I have her eating, but it's so exciting to be able to know I had a part in saving this little lamb. I had no idea country living could be so satisfying."

Rowdy's heart warmed. He'd just shared an important part of his world with Ange, and she'd appreciated it.

Maybe even liked it.

"So, I've been thinking," Ange said as Miss Woolsey nursed off her bottle and Rowdy continued to enjoy holding baby Toby, who'd fallen asleep against his shoulder. "It's been nearly a week and we haven't heard a word about another envelope."

The ball of warmth in Rowdy's chest instantly hardened into ice and plunged into the pit of his stomach.

He'd thought they were making progress here as he taught Ange the ins and outs of ranch life, that they were doing exactly what Granny Frances had expected of them. He was even enjoying himself.

So much so that there were moments when he forgot the whole point was to get this—whatever *this* was— over and done with so he could claim Granny Frances's ranch as his own.

But somehow in the process he started to see—*feel*— tiny inroads into putting the past behind them. Like the sensation of Toby in his arms while Ange bottle-fed the lamb.

As it turned out, all Ange was interested in was the next envelope—moving ever forward so she and Toby could leave Serendipity and put country living behind them.

Of course that was what she wanted.

That was what he wanted, too, wasn't it?

So why was he finding it so difficult to remember the truth of why they were here and his own desire to move things forward toward his future?

Nothing had changed.

He was getting careless with his emotions, allowing Toby to sneak his way into his heart along with remnants of what he'd once felt for Ange.

Because it couldn't be more than that. There was nothing in the *present* about what he was feeling for her. Nothing new.

The first time Ange had left, she'd done so abruptly and without an explanation—although in his heart, he'd known why she had gone. It was because she deserved better than to be tied down to a cripple.

This time, she'd laid it all out for him. No surprises.

She would fulfill Granny Frances's last wishes, and then she would leave.

Ange had broken his heart once.

He would not let her do so a second time.

Chapter Six

Angelica finished feeding Miss Woolsey, washed the bottle out in the barn sink and scrubbed her arms clean, and then went to relieve Rowdy of Toby, thinking he'd probably had enough of baby duty by now.

Rowdy had become extraordinarily quiet during the last few minutes, and Angelica couldn't read the unusual expression on his face.

This morning had gone well and she would definitely call it a win. They'd probably saved Miss Woolsey's life. Much more satisfying than feeding chickens.

It was exhilarating work, and Angelica's adrenaline was still pulsing through her veins. She'd learned very quickly to appreciate what ranchers spent their life's work on.

Saving a baby lamb? Now that was work worthy of pursuing.

So what was up with Rowdy?

His attitude had gone from day to night with no apparent explanation.

Maybe he just needed to eat something. In her limited experience with men, they tended to get grouchy when their stomachs were rumbling. Josh had always been that way, as had her father.

Rowdy was *nothing* like either of those men, but it was worth a shot. Even if his mood had nothing to do with the fact that he was hungry, he was still probably hungry.

"Why don't we stop by Cup O' Jo's for some lunch?" she suggested brightly. "It's been a long morning and I'm starving. Plus, I'm buying."

If she'd expected a positive reaction, something to the effect of, "Thank you, yes," she would have been disappointed.

She *was* disappointed.

Rowdy didn't even answer. He just sat on the hay bale where he'd parked himself earlier to nurse Toby and frowned down at the baby.

What was Rowdy's problem, anyway?

They'd had a great morning, and she was just trying to be nice. He'd kept Granny's ranch running and her stock healthy when Granny could no longer do the work herself. He'd continued to take care of the stock even after Granny had passed. He'd helped Angelica out a lot during this past week—and he hadn't needed to do any of it.

He could have let her fail. It might even have worked in his favor. He was helping her because of his love for Granny, and because the land would eventually be his.

Buying him a tasty meal was the least she could do to repay him for all he'd done.

That would also give them the opportunity to speak to Jo about when they should be expecting the next envelope.

She realized this whole conversation had been going

on in her head and Rowdy hadn't answered her. Did he want to eat or not? She narrowed her gaze on him.

"Is there a problem here?"

"No. No problem."

He met her eyes, his gaze determined and his jaw set.

She recognized that look. He was being stubborn about something. The only question now was what he was getting his back up about.

She decided to ignore his odd behavior for the time being and instead suggested they head for the café.

"Do you want to ride together?" she asked.

He nodded. "I've got a few chores left to finish here afterward, anyway."

"Let's use my SUV, since I've already got the attachment for Toby's car seat on the seat belt."

His short grunt of agreement was apparently all she was going to get.

Rowdy continued to remain silent during the short drive to the café, staring out the passenger-side window with a pensive expression on his face.

She would have given far more than a penny for his thoughts. She considered everything that had happened that morning, trying to figure out what had changed, where Rowdy's attitude had vectored off course.

She came up with a big fat nothing.

That was one thing the years had taken from them—the ability for them to communicate with one another without words. She used to be able to tell what he was thinking, how he was feeling.

But now, nothing.

Unless he was purposefully shutting her out.

To her surprise, Rowdy's demeanor changed the moment he stepped into the café. Smiling, he greeted

Jo with a side hug and a big smooch on her wrinkled cheek, then told her they would seat themselves in his regular booth.

So his attitude was just for her benefit, then. The brooding was all about her.

She didn't know why she was surprised, much less disappointed.

After all of the things she had done to him, some of which, like his limp, permanently lingered, it was a wonder that he even spoke to her at all, much less helped her get a handle on temporarily running Granny's ranch.

When Jo approached with her scratch pad, Rowdy ordered his usual, and Angelica blindly ordered the same, not even knowing what Rowdy's standard lunch order was anymore.

He used to like grilled cheese on whole wheat bread with dill pickle spears on the side and bag of barbecue chips, but the last time she'd sat in Cup O' Jo's with Rowdy had been when they were in their early twenties, and his tastes had probably grown and changed as much as he had.

Angelica didn't miss the many furtive glances and hissed whispers directed at her. Apparently, she was still a pariah. No doubt people were wondering why she was sitting with Rowdy—and why he didn't just up and leave.

It was only then that she realized what harm she could be doing, why Rowdy might have been dragging his feet when she'd suggested lunch at the café.

She'd inadvertently put him in the spotlight, in the awkward position of being seen sharing a meal with his ex-fiancée, and not only that, but a woman with a history of being the town's black sheep.

She respected Rowdy too much to have purposefully placed him in such a position, to put him through this embarrassing ordeal, but it was too late to back out now.

What was done was done.

Now all she could hope for was to make the rest of the meal as painless as possible and get out of there as quickly as they could.

She unhooked Toby from the car seat she'd set next to her on the booth and held him against her shoulder, knowing everyone in the café had a good view of her precious son.

She was a single mother, and maybe she was all those things the town accused her of being. They could judge her if they wanted to. She certainly had made more than her fair share of mistakes, and she owned up to them all.

But she was *not* ashamed of Toby. As far as she was concerned, the whole world could take their fill of looking, witnessing firsthand just how very much she loved her son.

Jo returned with their food—grilled cheese on whole wheat bread with dill pickle spears on the side and two bags of barbecue chips.

Apparently, some things really hadn't changed.

Angelica didn't know why that conclusion reassured her, but it did.

"Let me take that sweet baby while y'all enjoy your meal," Jo said, loud enough for every patron in the café to hear her.

It wasn't a suggestion, and Angelica immediately transferred Toby to her arms, knowing her son couldn't be in safer care.

Jo was like a second mother to most of the town, and

any babies who entered her café were fair game for loving on and spoiling by the boisterous redhead.

But Jo taking Toby away and walking him around the café left Angelica alone with Rowdy as they ate. That was sure to stir up the buzz in the gossip hive, as if it wasn't enough that they'd made such an unforeseen spectacle of themselves at the auction.

At least people at the auction would have—*rightly*—assumed Rowdy had been taken off-guard and had no connection with Angelica, and that when Jo lassoed him and led him off the stage, only to deliver the rope into a stunned Angelica's hands, it wasn't Rowdy's fault at all.

The two of them sharing lunch together, though, in public and alone—now that was a sheep of a completely different color.

"I'm sorry," she whispered as Rowdy took a bite of his sandwich. "I didn't think."

Rowdy chewed and swallowed, then dabbed at his lips with his napkin.

"I'm not following."

"I understand now why you were dragging your feet in coming to the café with me today. You can't tell me you haven't noticed the way people are staring at us and whispering behind our backs."

"What did you expect, Ange?" His words were blunt but his tone was laced with gentleness. "You show up eight years after running out on me at the altar and you expect everyone to welcome you with open arms, no questions asked?"

"Of course not. I hadn't anticipated making a public appearance in town at *all*. But that ship sailed the moment I arrived at that stupid auction."

"The auction changed a lot of things," Rowdy agreed. "For both of us."

Angelica was just about ready to excuse herself and let Rowdy eat in peace when he did the most unimaginable thing ever.

He reached across the table and took her hand, locking their gazes as he did so.

Flabbergasted, she could do no more than remain captured by his blue eyes. Her heart stopped beating. Her breath stopped flowing.

What was he doing?

"Sometimes, the best way to face down a problem is to walk right through it. People have their opinions, and whether or not they change their minds is up to them."

"Face down your fear and walk right through it," she repeated. He made it sound so easy, when it was anything but. When her fears were even now staring at them and wondering what was happening between the two of them.

A corner of Rowdy's lips quirked up. "Walk right through it," he gently coaxed. "Unless the fear in question is Granny's Psycho Rooster, in which case I'd advise you to turn and run in the opposite direction."

They shared a laugh, but that only brought more attention from those seated around them.

Rowdy clicked his tongue against his teeth. "Sure, you can try to demonstrate all God has done in your life and how much becoming Toby's mother has altered your character for the better, but at the end of the day, folks will still think and feel what they want."

She realized she didn't care what people thought of her. They would change their opinions. Or not. It didn't matter.

But Rowdy? That was a whole other thing, and her heart warmed at his words.

Did *he* sense a change in her—alteration for the better, as he had said?

But this wasn't about her.

"It's not my reputation I'm worried about. Think about what this is doing to you."

She snatched her hand back and clasped her hands under the table.

"It was wrong of me to bring you here. You shouldn't be seen with me."

"It's not like you hog-tied me and dragged me in here with you. I'm my own man, and I make my own decisions."

And he'd decided to be seen with her?

"Despite the fact that people will be talking about you behind your back?" she pressed. "I know what that feels like, and it's not nice. At best they'll believe you're foolish and vulnerable for spending time with me again after all I've done to you."

"We both know what we're doing and why we're doing it, and that is nobody's business but ours. Speaking of which," he said as he shook out the last crumbs of his potato chips into his palm, "here comes Jo with Toby."

He funneled the chips into his mouth, chewed and swallowed before he finished his thought.

"And she's carrying an envelope."

Rowdy swallowed down the flood of panic that rose like molten lava as he read his and Ange's names scribbled on the front of the envelope.

Just like the last time. The message that had resulted

in more confusion than he'd ever felt in his life. He was an emotional basket case.

What now?

Oddly, Ange's expression mirrored his, as if she'd swallowed something too large and it had stuck in her throat despite repeated attempts to swallow.

And yet she'd been the one who'd suggested asking Jo for the next envelope—all the better to leave Serendipity in the dust again with, my dear.

And the sooner the better, in her view.

She should be elated.

But now that the envelope rested on the table between them, she didn't look so certain. In fact, she was staring at the thing as if it were a rattlesnake, poised and ready to strike at her.

Ange had given Jo a bottle with which to feed Toby, and the older woman was seated in a chair nearby—far enough away to lend them a semblance of privacy, but then again, not really.

She was close enough to hear their conversation if she wanted to, and Rowdy guessed she did. She obviously knew a lot more about the envelope trail than he did.

Was this it?

The last missive?

At this point, he had no way of knowing. He would have to find a moment to pull Jo aside and ask her straight out. But first, there was the as-yet-unopened envelope to deal with.

Rowdy tested his feelings, gently poking at his myriad emotions and vulnerabilities.

Good memories. Bad memories. The pain of heartbreak.

And then there was what was happening between them now.

Bonding. Laughing. Spending time with Toby.

A friendship?

Or was he kidding himself and wanted more?

Did he still want Ange and Toby to leave? Was there a tiny, well-buried part of him that hoped, however unlikely, that Ange would stay and make Granny's ranch her home?

He shook his head. Why would he even consider such a notion?

They had a long bridge to cross to get anywhere near the closure they both needed.

However long or short she intended to stay, they hadn't yet approached the tender but necessary subject about what had happened to send Ange literally galloping out of his life all those years ago. It was a conversation they needed to have, no matter what kind of choices Ange made for her future.

But first—the envelope.

He took a deep breath and let it out slowly. So far, the missives, however short and vague, had turned out to be fairly straightforward. Hopefully this one was, too.

Granted, teaching Ange about the work Granny Frances had spent her whole life doing was a pretty tall order, but even in the short term, it was doable. To a point.

Sheep. Chickens. Avoiding roosters.

Ange's first letter, merely inviting her to a picnic, had been only the tip of a very large iceberg hovering just beneath the surface. But they'd weathered that one, too.

"Jo is giving us the eye," Ange said in a stage whisper, leaning forward on her elbows.

"You mean the one that is telling us to hurry up already? The one that brooks no argument?"

Ange chuckled and nodded. "That would be the one."

"Guess we'd better get at it, then."

"I suppose so." Ange picked up the envelope and slid her finger under the seal.

Her breath was coming heavy and erratic, nearly as erratic as Rowdy's pulse, as he opened the single sheet of tri-folded printer paper and shook it out to read.

"Teach My Lambs."

"What is it with Granny Frances and three-word instructions?" he asked, frustration turning his voice into gravel.

Rowdy had hoped for more, something that they could clearly understand, for starters, and not have to guess as to its meaning.

And then, possibly, something that would keep Ange and Toby in town for a little while longer, at least long enough for him to work out his conflicting feelings toward her and her precious son.

"Okay, then," Ange said, letting out a breath. *"Picnic With Jo* was a picnic with Jo—more or less. *Feed My Sheep* was feeding sheep—and avoiding Psycho Rooster. So now we have *Teach My Lambs*. Teach them to do what, do you suppose?"

At a total loss, Rowdy snorted and shook his head.

"I'm a sheep farmer and I obviously have a strong bias toward them. I honestly care for my stock." He chuckled. "That said, sheep really aren't that smart. If I don't have one of my dogs constantly herding them and one sheep wanders off, the rest will dumbly follow. I've had pregnant ewes get confused and claim a lamb as their own when they haven't even given birth yet."

She shook her head. "And then there was the ewe who rejected one of her twin lambs. How can that even be possible? It still blows me away."

"I'll be honest. I can't think of much of anything we could teach the sheep. And this letter doesn't even mention *sheep*. It says *lambs*. That's just nuts."

In his mind, he was picturing trying to coax a lamb to jump through a ring or roll over or beg. Bank off a hay bale or do flips?

A *lamb*?

So not going to happen.

"I told Frances this note would be too cryptic for you," Jo said, suddenly appearing at their table. Clearly, she'd been waiting for this precise moment to approach and intervene.

"Scooch over, big guy." She used her ample hips to bump Rowdy farther into the booth and take a seat beside him.

Toby was now sleeping silently in Jo's arms, and Ange offered to put him back in his car seat, but Jo would have none of it.

"I don't have nearly enough opportunities to cuddle with such sweetness," she said, pressing a kiss to Toby's forehead. "You're going to have to pry him away from me before you leave. He has the most precious features, doesn't he? Those almond-shaped blue eyes are to die for. I know experts say it's just a reflex at his age, but I am positive he smiled at me earlier. Plumb takes my breath away."

Rowdy couldn't agree more. He might be turning upside down and backward trying to figure out his feelings for Ange, but he had no such problems when it came to

Toby. That little fella had Rowdy's heart wrapped tightly around the tiny thumb he was sucking.

Ange beamed at Jo's compliments about her son, but her expression morphed into a combination of confusion and frustration when her gaze returned to the letter in her hand.

She folded it back into thirds and tapped the corner on the tabletop.

"Obviously, this doesn't give us enough to go on. I'm currently working with Granny's sheep, with Rowdy's help, just like the last note suggested. But now she wants me to do what? Teach my newborn lambs how to sing the 'Star Spangled Banner'?"

He was startled at Ange's use of the word *my*.

She'd said *my* lambs, not Granny's. Did that mean she was taking mental ownership of the ranch work she'd been doing?

Jo chuckled. "Singing sheep. Now that's something I'd like to see."

"Rowdy said it won't be easy to teach a lamb any kind of trick," Ange continued. "Sheep apparently aren't as smart as some other farm animals are."

"But Granny Frances knew that," Rowdy inserted. "So why would she even want us to try? It makes no sense."

"Because, my sweet darlings, she isn't talking about your lambs," Jo said. "She had a much smarter type of animal in mind, though no doubt a good bit more unpredictable."

Amusement twinkled in Jo's eyes. She was thoroughly enjoying taking them on this little roller-coaster ride. Rowdy wished she'd just get to the point and tell them what they were supposed to be doing.

Maybe he could at least get a little something from her without all this game playing.

"You'll tell us when we've received the last envelope, right?"

Her gaze widened in surprise. "Why, of course, my dear. I wouldn't even dream of leaving you both hanging indefinitely. That wouldn't be fair to either one of you."

And yet, she was, saying the lambs in the current letter weren't lambs at all, but not giving so much as a hint as to what they were really talking about.

He realized in hindsight that he hadn't asked the right question to clarify the whole shenanigan. He should have asked how many notes were left, got a precise number so they could at least have some clue where they were on the Granny Frances's Last Wishes Continuum.

Too late now. Knowing that this letter wasn't the last—and ignoring that tiny part of him that was leaping for joy that Ange and Toby weren't going away quite yet—would have to be enough.

At the end of the day, no matter how many envelopes were involved, Ange and Toby *would* be going away. No doubt she was already thinking about Toby's future and the many benefits he would have in the big city that Serendipity simply didn't and couldn't offer. And rightly so.

Rowdy returned his thoughts to the present just as Ange prompted Jo with another question.

"So, the *lambs* we are supposed to teach are actually...?"

"People. Teenagers, to be exact," Jo crowed with laughter at the expressions on their faces.

Teenagers?

Rowdy nearly choked on his breath. What on earth

did Granny Frances think he'd be able to do with teenagers? That was so far out of his comfort zone—not to mention his skill set—that it might as well be dinosaurs he was being asked to teach.

And the question remained—teach *what*?

Maybe he'd been mistaken and the letter had only been addressed to Ange.

Rowdy turned the envelope over to check out the front side.

Nope.

There it was, in black and white. Rowdy's name scribbled right next to Ange's, followed by three exclamation points for good measure. Granny Frances had definitely not wanted them to be mistaken on this point.

Ange cleared her throat, so Rowdy knew he wasn't the only one at the table having a hard time breathing through this new revelation.

"Which teenagers, exactly, are we talking about? And the note says nothing about what we are supposed to teach them."

Rowdy was glad Ange had picked up the conversation and was ferreting out the details, because he was still stunned to silence.

"Frances was very involved in the youth group at church," Jo explained.

Rowdy already knew that, but he had no idea what she did when she was with them. Led them in Bible studies and service projects, presumably.

Hmm. They could manage to do that, he supposed, especially if Jo pointed the way for them.

Collect clothing for the needy, or help a neighbor harvest early crops in order to give some of the bounty to some of Serendipity's poorer residents. Maybe do some sort of summer missions project.

"Frances was spearheading the annual ranch rodeo for the Fourth of July."

The *ranch rodeo*?

Jo's words were a sucker punch right to Rowdy's gut, robbing him of breath.

His gaze shot to Ange. Her face had drained of color until she was as white as a sheet. Her mouth opened and her lips were quivering, but no words emerged.

"I know it's usually the ranch hands who compete," Jo continued, as if she hadn't taken note of their re-action, "but this year it's going to be the teens from church. She did most of the legwork before she got sick, but she wanted you two to make sure the event goes off without a hitch, if you'll pardon my pun."

Rowdy's hands fisted in his lap.

"You must be mistaken," he said through gritted teeth. "Granny Frances would never ask that of us."

"Oh, I'm not mistaken, and she did," Jo affirmed promptly. "And before you ask, she knew exactly what she was doing when she wrote this letter and she was completely in her right mind. So I suggest both of you cowboy up and get used to the idea, because this ranch rodeo isn't going to happen unless you two get it in gear."

Ange was staring at the tabletop as if she hoped it would open up and swallow her whole.

Rowdy shook his head and set his shoulders.

"Then I'm sorry, Jo. You have to know that up until today, Ange and I have done everything required of us in Granny Frances's directives. We love her and we want to honor her last wishes.

"But a ranch rodeo? That's just not going to happen."

Chapter Seven

Rowdy's response didn't surprise Angelica in the least, and she doubted Jo was shocked by it, either. But Granny's note had floored her as effectively as an uppercut to the jaw would have done.

Fortunately, she was already seated, or the lurch her stomach took might have sent her reeling. And she was glad Jo still held on to Toby. Angelica didn't want her sweet son picking up on the maelstrom of emotions sweeping like a hurricane through her chest.

A ranch rodeo?

How could Granny have even considered such a thing?

Not for Angelica and Rowdy.

The ranch rodeo was a yearly event in Serendipity, where local ranchers competed in laugh-out-loud-hilarious events like wild cow milking and paint branding as they mimicked the work they did on the ranch.

"You both owe her so much," Jo inserted, as if in response to Angelica's thoughts—and Rowdy's white-faced expression. "I don't have to remind you that these are her last wishes. Ya gotta do what ya gotta do, no matter how painful it gets."

"Yes, but—" Angelica didn't know how to finish her response, so she let it drop. Her eyes flew to Jo, who nodded as if the matter was settled.

Angelica switched her gaze to Rowdy, who appeared even more befuddled than she was—and angry, as well he should be. His whiskered cheeks darkened to a deep cherry and worry lines creased his forehead.

Granny should never have asked this of him.

For once, Angelica could really see his age, and the effects of all the stress he'd had to endure, including the many ways she'd hurt him.

"You know what you have to do," Jo reminded them. "Frances's plans are in the top drawer of her filing cabinet in her home office. The youth group meets on Sunday afternoons, which means you'll only have a couple of sessions between now and the day of the ranch rodeo to sort out who is doing what and when. We've been rotating teachers from the congregation to fill in for their weekly meetings, but now that you're here you can take over.

"Frances won't be the only one you'd be letting down. The kids will be so disappointed if you don't step up and help them make this rodeo a success. And you only have two weeks to plan."

That was one last jab Angelica didn't need.

"Granny Frances couldn't have meant that she wanted us there," Rowdy protested. "She knew I never attended the Fourth of July activities, and I especially avoided the ranch rodeos. Everyone in town knows why."

Angelica's breath left her in a whoosh and her heart felt as if it was being squeezed by an invisible fist.

The fallout of Rowdy's statement, the emotional shrapnel, rained over her.

Picnicking with Jo, even if she had ended up in the middle of a town crowd she had very much wished to avoid, and even learning how to work a sheep farm—those were doable, if difficult, tasks.

But organizing and overseeing a ranch rodeo?

Now, that was just plain cruel.

Angelica and Rowdy—especially Rowdy—ought to get up and walk away right now.

She hated to disappoint the teens in the youth group, but one year without a rodeo wouldn't be the end of the world for Serendipity and the teenagers would have many more opportunities to compete in future ranch rodeos.

Besides, there were plenty of other activities for townsfolk to enjoy on the Fourth of July—music, a rope obstacle course for the kids, community games and of course fireworks to end the evening with a bang.

"I know this will be difficult—for both of you," she acknowledged. "But I really think it's important. Important enough for Frances to make this request of you."

"Yeah, but to what end?" Rowdy muttered as his eyebrows furrowed.

"What benefit could she possibly foresee?" Angelica asked, pressing further. "To me, the whole suggestion is a recipe for disaster."

"I'm inclined to agree with you," Jo said, although the determined spark in her eyes said otherwise. "When you've finished your meal, go back to Frances's ranch and read through the plans she left you. Maybe they will clue you in as to why she's chosen you to complete this difficult task."

In the next moment, Jo transformed from an attitude of serious concern to that of bubbly enthusiasm.

"Anyone up for some New York cheesecake?" she asked brightly. "Phoebe's been working on them all morning. She's actually from New York, did you know?"

Phoebe Hawkins was the local pastry chef who'd transplanted from New York City. She'd had a stellar national reputation, and had left everything to marry Chance, the café's cook and Jo's nephew. And she couldn't have been happier.

At any other time, Angelica wouldn't even have considered passing up one of Phoebe's delectable treats, but right now her stomach was in knots and she was feeling a tad nauseated.

Rowdy's eyes met hers and he gave her a nearly imperceptible nod.

"I think we'll pass on dessert today," Rowdy said, speaking for both of them. "It sounds like we have a lot to work out back at Granny Frances's office, and I know we're both anxious to see what's what on this ranch rodeo and make some decisions on where to go from here."

"Of course, dear. Just remember, that envelope Angelica's holding is an important component of Frances's last wishes. Don't let her down."

They got the message already. Angelica didn't think Jo needed to keep rubbing it in.

Angelica collected Toby and locked him in his car seat, then followed Rowdy out to her SUV.

"I'll take *ignoring the guilt card* for five hundred dollars, please," she remarked the moment they were alone in the vehicle together. She couldn't help feeling slightly snarky about it all.

"Jo did pour it on pretty thick," he agreed, then fell silent.

The ride back to Granny's ranch was made in the same uncomfortable quiet as the ride to the café had been—Rowdy staring out the window in brooding silence and Angelica driving with her jaw set and both hands clenched on the steering wheel, trying to breathe through her frustration.

When they reached the ranch, Angelica suggested she put Toby down for his afternoon nap while Rowdy went to the office to see if he could find the file Jo was talking about.

She sensed Rowdy's hesitation well before he spoke.

"Would it be too much to ask for me to be the one who puts Toby down and for you to go find the file?"

Angelica was nearly as reluctant to revisit the past through the contents of Granny's file as Rowdy was.

But she thought it might be better for them to face it *together*.

"Why don't we both put Toby down and then go find the file?" she suggested gently.

What had Granny been thinking?

She'd been asking that question a lot since she'd returned to Serendipity, but instead of finding answers she kept running into more questions.

Not to mention confused feelings.

Thanks to Granny, she had gone from never, *ever* intending to see Rowdy again to working with him on a daily basis. And now, they were standing together in Toby's nursery preparing the baby for his nap, making the area feel oddly intimate.

Rowdy's large figure took up more than just area in the room. He took up emotional space, as well.

Angelica's pulse was pounding as she changed Toby, and she knew by the way the baby's feet and arms flapped that he was picking up on her discomfort. She took a deep breath and tried to calm the frantic beat of her heart.

Rowdy noticed Toby's disquiet, as well.

"Does the little guy need a bottle or something before we lay him down in his crib?"

Angelica shook her head. "He just needs to be rocked for a minute."

Rowdy came up behind her. He wasn't quite touching her, but she could feel his warm presence as tangibly as if he'd put his arms around her and pulled her close to him.

"May I?" His voice was low and scratchy.

Rowdy picked up Toby and laid him against his broad shoulder, then sang a soft lullaby in a rich baritone while shuffling his cowboy boots around the room in an unchoreographed dance.

Angelica hadn't even known Rowdy could sing, and it occurred to her only now that there were probably many things she didn't know about the man Rowdy had become.

The boy she remembered was not the man who now stood before her—and not just physically, either.

Eight years of living had changed and molded him, just as it had done with her.

But as he bent over the crib to put the now-sleeping Toby to bed, lingering there for a moment with a tender, appreciative expression on his face, it wasn't the past or the present Angelica was considering.

It was the future.

Or at least, the future that might have been if she

hadn't ruined everything. For one moment, she allowed herself to compare the differences.

Rowdy as her spouse and her soul mate.

Toby as their son.

But those things were not and could not ever be true.

She had to close the door on this way of thinking and all of the emotions such imaginings invoked, or she would drive herself crazy.

And she knew exactly how to close the door on the past and the future.

Permanently.

By opening the ranch rodeo file in Granny's office cabinet.

Rowdy was literally dragging his booted feet as Ange lead him into Granny Frances's office.

He had just experienced one of the most incredible, special moments of his life—getting to participate in an important ritual for baby Toby.

With the three of them taking up the majority of the room in the small nursery, which was furnished with only a crib and a changing table, sharing the space together felt intimate in a way he'd never before experienced.

The comparisons between what was and what could have been didn't escape him.

But for possibly the first time since Ange had re-entered his life, he didn't run from those thoughts and emotions.

Toby was such a precious little soul, with so much life teeming from those almond-shaped blue eyes and the heart-capturing smile that only a Down baby could make.

When he'd commented on it, Ange had laughed and

said that at Toby's age it was only a reflex smile, but Rowdy still couldn't help but believe the baby's grin was just for him.

As for Toby's mama—he wasn't quite ready to confront all his feelings for Ange, much less contemplate what that might mean for them in the future.

Not that there would be a future of *any* kind for the three of them after they'd taken a look at the contents of Granny Frances's file. Neither one of them even wanted to revisit the past, to think about ranch rodeos, never mind plan one. Rowdy, because of his injury, and Ange, who had jilted him because she couldn't handle the thought of living with a man who might always be bound to a wheelchair.

She'd left without knowing he'd be able to walk again.

But then, he'd told her to leave.

There were too many bad memories.

Part of him just wanted to turn around and walk out without knowing what Granny Frances expected of him, but despite realizing how disruptive the file might be, he couldn't walk away.

Would the contents change everything between him and Ange, when they would have to plan a saddle bronc riding event—especially with teenagers as the participants? With the thought that someone might be injured, just as Rowdy had been all those years ago?

Rowdy hadn't attended a ranch rodeo since his injury, but he knew there hadn't been any accidents since. Even his had been a freak calamity that no one could have foreseen.

There was no reason to think this year would be different. And yet a cloud of doubt hovered over him, and he suspected it hung over Ange, as well.

By the end of today, it might not be him walking away from whatever tentative feelings were growing between them.

Ange might take Toby and *run*.

Upon first entering the office, Ange placed the baby monitor she'd taken with her from the nursery on the edge of the desk, so both of them would hear Toby when he woke from his nap.

After wrestling to open the rusty top drawer of the battered metal file cabinet, she immediately drew out a bright yellow accordion file folder stuffed with papers, some with bent corners sticking out of the top.

Granny Frances was many things, but organized wasn't one of them, at least with her paperwork. She hated that part of owning a ranch and avoided it whenever she could.

Rowdy had visited Granny Frances in her office from time to time, and bills and receipts had always littered the desktop with no rhyme or reason that he could see, although Granny Frances had insisted that she had a system that worked for her.

The bills and receipts were gone now. Jo and Granny Frances's lawyer must have been in here as part of settling the estate.

And yet they had left this one file.

"It's the only thing in here," Ange confirmed when he asked. She used two hands to move the awkwardly large file to the center of the desk.

She took a seat in Granny Frances's office chair and he sat on the opposite side of the desk.

Their gazes locked as Ange removed the thick pile of papers and fanned them out across the desk.

Rowdy knew they were both thinking the same thing—the one and only ranch rodeo he'd ever participated in had been the beginning of the end of their relationship.

Ange cleared her throat and riffled through the pages. "Every youth whose family owns a ranch is a team leader. The kids whose parents work in the community or as ranch hands have all been assigned as seconds. From the look of it, we're going to have at least twelve ranches participating, maybe more."

"We? I haven't agreed to anything yet."

"I know." Her lips curled downward.

"Have you found a list of events yet?" he asked.

She shook her head. "It's not anywhere on these first few pages. Let's see."

She continued to rifle through the papers and eventually pulled one from the center of the bunch. "Here it is—although this looks more like Granny was brainstorming than anything that was set in stone. There are doodles all over the page. It appears to be a mind map of sorts."

"So, what have we got?"

He knew he was speaking through gritted teeth and he tried to relax his jaw, but the more he concentrated on relaxing, the more his muscles tightened. His fisted hands were grasping the edge of his chair in a death grip.

"The usual." She was trying to keep her tone light and even, but he could hear her voice shaking and knew she was going to say *those words* before they ever crossed her lips.

"We've got stray gathering, trailer loading, paint branding, wild cow milking and mutton busting." She paused. "That's always a good one to get the crowd laughing."

He didn't buy her upbeat tone for a second.

"And?" he asked, his mouth dry and his voice coarse.

She dropped her gaze from his.

"And saddle bronc riding."

There.

The words had been said and were now hanging in the air between them.

Saddle bronc riding.

The injury he'd sustained competing in that event was the reason he still walked with a limp to this day.

And it was likewise the reason Ange had ultimately chosen to run away from him before their wedding.

Granny Frances had used three words to communicate her wishes in the notes she had left for them.

But these three words weren't anything like Granny Frances's kind, if cryptic, notes.

They were pure poison, damaging Rowdy and Ange in a way no other words could do.

Saddle bronc riding.

Chapter Eight

A ngelica's heart nearly split in two as she watched the pain and agony that crossed over Rowdy's expression before his face hardened.

He must be reliving his accident.

All of it.

She wouldn't blame him if he stood up and flipped the desk over before stalking off in a rage, not that Rowdy would ever make such a display of fury.

He wasn't that man.

But he *should* be angry.

As for Angelica, she had a big fat *guilty* stamped on her forehead in permanent black ink.

She waited for Rowdy to speak, but he didn't. He just snapped the page from her grasp and gave it a long perusal, his hand running across the stubble on his jaw.

"We don't have to keep the saddle bronc riding event," she suggested gently. "We don't *have* to be in charge of this rodeo at all."

Rowdy hissed an audible breath through his teeth.

"Surely with Jo's help we can find someone else to pull this together," she continued. "Someone who doesn't have the kind of history with it as we do. I don't care what Jo said earlier. She would understand why we can't do this."

Rowdy remained silent and thoughtful for a moment, then shook his head.

"Granny Frances wanted *us* to do it. And she knew at least as well as anyone did what kind of history she would be digging up with this request."

"I think I'm beginning to understand where at least part of this scavenger hunt, or whatever you want to call it, is coming from."

"Yeah?"

"Granny was the only one from my old life who I kept in touch with at all," she explained. "And that was only near the end of the eight years I was gone, after I discovered I was pregnant with Toby. That was when I finally reached out to her. When I left Serendipity, I left everything and everyone behind, even Granny."

He grunted in response, leaning back in his chair and crossing his arms.

"After I calmed down and realized what I'd done in running away from our wedding, my mindless fear disappeared and guilt readily took its place. Oh, Rowdy, I am so ashamed of my actions, especially the many ways I hurt you. I truly believed you were the love of my life and the man I wanted to marry. I shouldn't have left the way I did. I should have treated our relationship—and you—with more respect."

Rowdy visibly flinched, his face coloring with emotion.

"Do we have to dig all this up again?"

"Yes. I believe we do. It seems to me that all of this—" she made a grand gesture that spanned far be-

yond just the office and into the entirety of the ranch
and beyond "—was done in order to force us to coop-
erate, to work out some of our issues."

She waited for his response, her stomach queasy
and her face so enflamed it must be at least as red as
Rowdy's.

He stood and stalked to the office door, and for a
moment she thought he was leaving but then he turned
back and walked in her direction. He planted his fists
on the desktop and leaned toward her.

"Why would she do that?" His voice was a gravel-
sounding mixture of confusion and anger. "Why force
the issue?"

"Honestly, I think, at least for me, she was ripping
off the bandage to allow my wounds to heal naturally.
To heal my heart."

He looked genuinely perplexed.

"Wounds? What wounds? From where I'm standing,
you're the one who did all the ripping." He growled in
frustration. "You walked out on *me*, remember?"

How could she not?

It had been on her mind every day since the night
it happened.

From the time she'd agreed to follow Granny's missives that included spending time with Rowdy, she'd
known this conversation was bound to happen. All of
this—staying in Serendipity, discovering Granny's intentions and God's had led her here to this moment.

She wanted to flee from the office and avoid a con-
frontation, but that was her old self.

Her new self, with the Lord's help, would seek to
make amends for all of the pain and suffering she'd

caused Rowdy, and seek closure for both of them so they could move on with their lives.

"I did walk out on you," she admitted, folding her hands on the desk and tilting her head up until their gazes met. "Rode off, actually."

That last part was her attempt to insert a note of dry humor into the conversation.

Epic fail.

"But I think we need to go back a little bit further than that," Ange said.

Rowdy's brow furrowed. "What's that supposed to mean?"

"Granny never had a mean bone in her body, so it makes no sense that she would ask us to revisit the ranch rodeo and all the painful memories from it unless she truly felt we needed to begin there and move forward."

Rowdy didn't move a muscle, as if he'd turned to ice.

"If I don't miss my guess, the saddle bronc riding is where she wanted us to start. We have to decide whether or not we want to keep the event in our lineup, which by default means we have to face up to what happened eight years ago. We need to talk about it. Perhaps try to find some kind of closure."

She hitched a breath but it stuck in her throat. "Except there is no closure. Not for you. Not with your—"

She couldn't finish the sentence. Tears pricked at the backs of her eyes and it took every ounce of her willpower not to let them go, knowing if she did she wouldn't be able to keep from sobbing in earnest.

"My limp. You can say it, Ange. I've had eight years to get used to the idea. It hardly bothers me anymore, and I don't mind talking about how I got the injury."

"Does it still hurt?" Angelica pulled her bottom lip

between her teeth and bit down hard enough to taste the copper of her own blood. The pain distracted her from her shredding heart.

"No. Not really. It aches a little when we have a cold snap or if I crouch one too many times in a day. Nothing that taking an anti-inflammatory can't fix."

"But you walk with a limp."

"I'll never be at one hundred percent. My leg drags a little when I'm not paying attention or I get too tired. But again, I've learned to live with it and it doesn't bother me. Honestly."

He sat down and rolled his shoulders. "My muscles ache more from daily ranch work than from a rodeo injury that happened years ago."

Angelica couldn't help the way her gaze took him in—his broad shoulders sloping to a lean waist. A well-muscled chest and firm biceps carved from a life of picking up hay bales and feed sacks. Strong legs from walking endless fields and riding horses.

He had no need of a gym. His lifestyle was quite enough to keep him in tip-top condition.

He tilted his head and caught her gaze, and she realized she'd been caught staring—and not only that, but caught staring *appreciatively*.

A spark of humor lit his blue eyes and the heat in her face became a bonfire. Her pulse raced, and it wasn't just because she'd been caught, nor that Rowdy had clearly followed the train of her thoughts.

She was reacting to him.

The man sitting just across the desk from her.

Not the boy who'd believed in her when no one else would give her a chance, nor even the one whose life she'd wrecked with her careless words and actions.

Just Rowdy, the cowboy Granny had recently sent her off on an adventure with.

An adventure they were far from having finished.

She hated to douse the spark in his eyes, or bring the stress back when he'd just now started to relax. His body language said it all.

Suddenly, the baby monitor crackled to life as Toby wakened. Angelica excused herself long enough to bring Toby and his bouncer into the office.

By this time, Rowdy was slumped back in his seat with one ankle crossed over the other knee. The muscles in his shoulders had loosened and he'd laced his fingers over his flat stomach.

"We still have to talk about this," she said, avoiding his gaze.

"Yeah. We do."

Of course. Ange had hit the nail right on the head.

Confronting the past. Laying to rest every nightmare that lingered. Not only revisiting it, but closing that chapter so they could both move on with their lives.

Move on.

He with an expanded acreage and an increase in stock. Ange and Toby with enough money to see them settled for at least the immediate future. Maybe Ange could even start a trust fund for Toby's long-term care out of the sale of Granny Frances's ranch.

A win-win for everyone concerned.

So why didn't it feel like a win to him?

"The accident," he said grimly.

When their eyes had met a moment ago, he'd been certain she'd been giving him a flattering once-over, which only served to make his own attraction for her more undeniable as his pulse quickened.

Some of her allure was her pretty face and hourglass figure, but that wasn't everything.

He'd been drawn to her from the moment they entered kindergarten and she'd been sent to the principal's office on the first day of school for fighting.

Rowdy had seen the whole thing and he knew what had really happened. Ange had stepped into the middle of an unfair struggle with a big bully of a girl who had pushed another, smaller girl to the ground at recess and was pulling her hair until the little girl was screaming in pain.

The other girl had gotten away with nothing more than a reprimand. Ange had come out of the escapade with a black eye and detention, despite the little girls she'd rescued coming to her defense. The situation was made worse by the fact that she was the pastor's daughter and consequently held to a higher standard of behavior.

And yet she'd never said a word to defend her own actions.

Ange was a scrappy little thing, defending the defenseless and taking the brunt of the blame with no care for herself.

Whenever good-little-Christian Rowdy stepped in to help, he was praised, whereas Ange, who defied her faith and her parents, was unfairly criticized, all because teachers and staff had labeled her a troublemaker.

By high school, she was understandably rebellious, skipping school and hanging out with a bad crowd, while Rowdy, though he struggled with academics, was a model student who worked his sheep farm alongside his parents rather than participate in extracurricular activities or sports.

It was Granny Frances who had originally set him up with Ange, inviting both of them to her house at the same time and then acting as if it hadn't been planned. And though on paper a relationship between Rowdy and Ange should never have worked, it did.

Or at least, it had.

Until he got injured at that wretched ranch rodeo. He shouldn't have been saddle bronc riding in the first place. But he'd been young and stupid and had believed, as most youth did, that he was invincible.

"You're right," he acknowledged, knowing that Ange had been waiting for his response. "The ranch rodeo changed everything for us."

She flinched and her lips pressed into a thin, straight line. She squeezed her eyes closed and he wondered if she was holding back tears.

His own eyes were burning as he took a deep breath and plunged into the deep.

"You—you were right to call off the wedding."

There.

He'd said it aloud, words that he had never even dared to admit to himself, much less tell another.

It had been so much easier to point the finger at Ange and harbor resentment toward her than to take the responsibility that belonged only to him.

The truth was so much more complicated than casting blame.

"I was wrong to—" Ange started, but then her words skidded to a halt midsentence. "What did you say?"

This time he didn't stutter or falter in his words.

"I said you were right not to marry me."

Hurt and shock crossed her expression.

"What?"

"You only did what I told you to do. I was the one who said we ought to break it off before the wedding."

"And you meant it?"

He shook his head. "No. I was immature and resentful about my injury. I believed I wasn't any good to anyone, especially you. I didn't know if I would ever walk again, and I couldn't ask you to tie yourself to a man in a wheelchair. I couldn't provide for you if I couldn't work the ranch."

"How could you even think that?" she asked, her voice strained. "I was ready to recite vows that included for better or for worse."

"No marriage should start with *worse*."

"What?" she squeaked.

"Didn't you have your doubts?"

"Of course I did. But not about you being in a wheelchair. Like you said, we were both young and immature. I doubted myself, not you."

"If you did, it was because I hadn't offered you the support you needed to believe in yourself. I was focused on myself, on regaining my own strength, and in the process, I shut you out."

"That's not it at all. I'm talking about how you got injured in the first place. Rowdy, I was *responsible* for your accident. You wouldn't have been on that horse at all if it wasn't for me. You got hurt because of me."

He stared at her in confusion, utterly bewildered.

"You don't even remember, do you?" She sounded flabbergasted. "I dared you to do the saddle bronc riding—pressured you into it, even when you told me that saddle bronc riding wasn't really your thing. If it wasn't for me, you wouldn't have participated. You wouldn't have ridden that bronc, and you wouldn't have had that accident."

She scoffed. "Stupid me. Saddle bronc riding is the most dangerous event in ranch rodeo, and I wanted my fiancé to show off and win so that *I* could have bragging rights. I didn't give a second's thought as to what I might be doing to you. Some loving fiancée I was. It still makes me sick just to think about it."

Rowdy frowned. "How many times do I have to tell you this? I am my own man and I always have been. I wouldn't have signed up for that event unless I wanted to."

"Yes, but that's my point. *Why* did you want to ride? It was because I kept bringing it up and encouraging you to sign up. I wouldn't take no for an answer."

He jerked his head in acknowledgment. "That was part of it. I thought I had something to prove to you, something that riding a bronc would do. But I had something to prove to myself, as well.

"I've always lived a fairly isolated life out on my ranch, even when I was a teenager. I never played sports or did any extracurricular activities. I saw the ranch rodeo as something I could do to become more involved with the community, and maybe I had something to prove to the cattle ranchers. The Triple X Ranch needed a saddle bronc rider, and none of their wranglers wanted to tackle it, so I signed up."

"Even though bronc riding wasn't in your skill set. The point of a ranch rodeo is to mimic the work wranglers actually perform on their ranches. Starting and training horses is a big part of the work on some ranches, but not yours. You never rode broncs."

She sighed. "You would have been better served in an event like paint branding or trailer loading. And you might be the best man in town at stray gathering."

"It sounds foolish and not at all well thought through when you put it that way," he admitted. "But I was nearly twenty-one, in prime physical condition, and I was on top of my world. My dreams were coming true. I was about to marry the most wonderful woman I'd ever known and then we were going to settle down and raise a wonderful family on the land I loved. I got cocky, and then I got hurt."

"I still think I'm to blame," Angelica insisted. "I was the one who put the idea in your head in the first place."

"Maybe so, but there is no way you could have foreseen what would happen. It was a freak accident. Everyone said so, including the saddle bronc experts. My horse panicked and hit the wall, crushing my knee. I couldn't have seen it coming, nor could I have responded quickly enough to have avoided the collision, especially since my focus was on getting to the end of those eight seconds any way I could. I didn't know what my horse was going to do."

He scrubbed a hand across his jaw. "At the end of the day, I rode because I wanted to show off for you. But it wasn't your fault I got hurt."

Toby made a mewling sound from his bouncer, which Rowdy now recognized as his precursor to crying.

"What is it, little man? You think you need to be part of this conversation?" Ange lifted Toby into her arms.

"I know I was a jerk to you after the accident," Rowdy said. "In my anger and frustration at being crippled, I pushed you away."

"You did push me away, but I should never have

gone. I understood your exasperation at being confined to a wheelchair. You are a man of the land, and not being able to do your ranch work must have made you feel inadequate.

"Yet no injury of any kind should ever have pulled me from your side."

She paused and ran a hand across her cheek as if to wipe away a tear. "I never told you how much I admired your determination to work through the pain of physical therapy. I know it wasn't easy for you."

"I'm a proud man," he acknowledged. "Too proud, sometimes. I should have let you in, dealt with this crisis together as a couple should, and instead I told you that you didn't want to marry a cripple. The fact that I didn't really mean the words doesn't negate the fact that they were said."

"I wanted to marry *you*, Rowdy. Like I said before. For better or for worse."

"Then why did you run away?"

Angelica stared down at Toby for a moment, as if searching for the right words with which to answer his question.

At last, she hitched in a breath and plunged forward.

"Because I was afraid."

Rowdy's brow furrowed and he scrubbed a hand through his thick hair.

"And I heard you."

"You heard me? You heard me *what*?"

"Laughing. Joking around with your groomsmen after the wedding rehearsal."

"On the day before our wedding? Of course I was laughing. I was elated, over the moon with joy."

Her face flushed a furious red. "You don't understand."

"Then enlighten me."

"You'd been so cross and moody since your accident, which was nothing like you. And as I said, I blamed myself for that.

"I know we were getting along better as our wedding day approached, but we were still working out our problems. When I heard you with your groomsmen, you sounded so happy and carefree. Far more than you'd been with me at any time after the accident."

All this time, he had thought Ange had left him because she'd realized he wasn't good enough for her, that he couldn't provide for her. That she didn't want to be saddled with a man who was less than one hundred percent.

But now he realized it was far more complicated than he'd could ever have imagined.

Ange had dropped her gaze and was nuzzling Toby's neck, whispering soft reassurances that Rowdy suspected were as much for her benefit as they were for Toby's.

"You heard me laughing," he repeated, his throat tightening around the words. "Honey, you should have said something if it bothered you."

"I know that now. But back then, I wasn't strong enough to face you. I wanted you to be happy, truly happy, and I convinced myself I was the last woman in the world who could give you that joy. I had suspected it for a long time and my fear grew until it overwhelmed me. I realized how wrong the two of us were together. Whether I'd meant to or not, I'd hurt you by insisting you ride in that ranch rodeo, and I knew I was bad news for you.

Maybe it would have been something different, but something else would have happened, again and again. I'm no good for you."

Fresh tears welled in her eyes. Toby made a distressed mewl. Even though he was only a few weeks old, Toby could tell something was wrong. He didn't like his mama sad and crying.

Rowdy didn't want that, either. He picked up a stuffed blue bunny from the bouncer and reached for Toby, giving Ange a moment to compose herself.

He hummed a few bars of a Texas two-step and shuffled and danced around the room with Toby, who appeared to love the attention and the rhythm of the song and dance.

"Don't you think I should have been the judge of that?" he asked between beats.

"Yes. I see that now. But back then I was afraid that if I talked to you, you would convince me to stay, and that was the one thing I couldn't do—not when I believed I wasn't the right person for you to share your life with. I wrongly assumed that after I left, you probably thanked God every day that you hadn't been saddled with someone so inherently wrong for you. Someone who would *not* be a good partner to you in your daily work and life."

"But we talked about that, how you would contribute to running the ranch. Though of course things had changed after the accident. I couldn't do my work, and my church friends couldn't keep running my ranch in my absence forever. Is that what it was?" Because that was the only conclusion that made sense to Rowdy, then or now.

"Injured or not, I didn't come from a ranching background. I had been deluding myself to think I could truly be a life mate to you, to contribute in a way that would make you proud. My life has been a series of one mistake after another. Eventually, I would have dragged you down with me."

"I don't believe that," he said, his voice the consistency of gravel.

"I should have trusted in my love for you," Ange said at last. "I let my hurt feelings get in the way of my good judgment. You'll never know how sorry I am."

Rowdy thought he might.

Because he was sorry, too.

Sorry that she'd judged herself and had come up wanting, when she was nothing like the person she saw in the mirror.

Sorry he hadn't lent her the strength and courage to believe in herself, to see what he saw every time he looked at her.

He'd known that underneath the tough exterior she presented to the world, she was soft and vulnerable. And he hadn't protected her enough to let that part of her personality see the light of day.

Ange sighed. "If only things had turned out differently. Maybe there would have been hope for the two of us. But it's too late now. We made our choices and we have to live with them."

Rowdy wasn't sure he agreed with that last bit.

Yes, they had lost each other in the past, but did that necessarily mean there was no chance for them in the future? Not starting over, exactly, nor picking up where they left off. Too much had happened and too many years had passed for that.

But what about tentatively exploring something new between them, a relationship that not only encompassed the two of them, but Toby, as well?

And God.

The Lord had been missing from their equation back then, but He would be at the forefront of any new relationship they built together.

He studied Ange, wondering if he should suggest they make no permanent decisions until they'd had more time to let all of these new revelations sink in, but she had already shut down, her expression stoic and determined.

He'd seen that look before, and there was no getting through it.

"We'd better get to planning if we're going to get this ranch rodeo up and running by the Fourth of July," she said in a patently false tone.

Rowdy's chest felt like it was being squeezed in a vise. Ange was doing what she always did when confronted with something she didn't want to hear—pulling back into herself and blocking everything and everybody else out.

And after that, it wouldn't be long before she ran away, just as she'd done on the night of their wedding rehearsal.

But this time, Rowdy would anticipate her move. He didn't know what the future held for them, but one thing he did know—

He wasn't going to let her skip out of his life again.

Chapter Nine

Early on the third day of July, with Toby comfortably sleeping in his stroller a few feet away, Angelica directed Rowdy as he guided his empty horse trailer into the correct position inside Serendipity's town arena. He parked it close to one wall, since trailer loading was an event that didn't require as much moving space as some of the others.

The goal was for the cowboy or cowgirl two-person teams to get their horses into and out of the trailer in the fastest time. The trick was, the horses provided were barely started and mostly unfamiliar with being loaded into the big trailer.

Many contestants got inventive when the horses balked, as they inevitably did, and the event was always a true crowd-pleaser.

The whole ranch rodeo carried with it much laughter and amusement. And there were no trophies or monetary awards for the winners. The ranch hands entertained the audience only for their pleasure and attempted to win events merely for yearly bragging rights.

But none of this felt *fun* to Angelica.

For a moment, she mentally shook her fist at Granny for putting her in this situation. Angelica knew that what Granny had done, she had done out of love for her and Rowdy, but her plan had backfired. Granny was no longer around, and Angelica was left with the fallout.

She ached. So deeply and profoundly that nothing could come close to matching it, with the possible exception of the night she'd ridden away from Serendipity on a horse that was supposed to be her bridal transportation.

She and Rowdy had worked up a planned list of events from Granny's notes, and now they were setting everything up in the arena for the next day.

After parking the trailer, they moved on to create a "branding" station—paint buckets filled with blue, green and red paints. On a nearby table were branding irons specific to each competing ranch.

"Do you think we've got enough paint, or should we stop by Emerson's Hardware and grab some extra to keep on standby?" she asked.

"Yes," Rowdy said, his mind clearly elsewhere— probably revisiting the past.

"Yes, we have enough paint, or yes, we need more?"

"What?" he asked, his gaze fixing on hers. One side of his lips crept up in a half-smile. "Yes, I think we have enough paint," he said.

He was silent for a full minute as they marked chalk lines the teens would have to keep their cows within as they attempted to "brand" them.

Then he turned to her, swiping off his black cowboy hat and exposing his thick blond curls.

"So that event is ready. And I've corralled the sheep from your ranch that we'll need for the mutton busting." Angelica's stomach fluttered when she realized the verbal slip he'd made, calling the ranch hers and not Granny's.

Well, it was Granny's ranch, whatever he said, and someday soon it would be his. So much had happened between her and Rowdy that it was getting harder and harder to remember that.

"Let's take a break before we set up the rest of the events. We won't be bringing in any of the stock until tomorrow morning. I'll help you load a few sheep into your trailer for the mutton busting. I'm picking up a couple of wild cows, Nick McKenna has offered some of his cattle for the herding and branding events and his brother Jax and his wife are bringing in some saddle broncs."

She watched his face as he talked about the saddle broncs, noting the momentary glimpse of agony that flashed through his eyes.

"We can still remove saddle bronc riding from the program," she said, as she'd mentioned several times previously.

She wasn't sure *she* could handle the event. She couldn't imagine how Rowdy, who'd sustained a permanent injury from it that changed his whole life, would deal with it.

He met her gaze squarely.

"No." His voice was firm and unwavering. "Saddle bronc riding has been a treasured part of Serendipity's ranch rodeo for as long as I can remember. It's a big draw, not to mention the most adrenaline-fueled event."

"I should think so, since the rest of the events are meant to be more humorous than skilled."

His lips quirked. "Well, it does take some level of skill to milk a wild cow."

She couldn't help but chuckle.

"Tomorrow, we'll need to do a sound check on the system Frank and Jo Spencer will be using to officiate," he said.

He stroked a hand across his jaw, as he often did when he was thinking, leaving multicolored finger streaks of chalk across his cheek.

Angelica couldn't help it. She put a palm over her mouth and giggled.

His eyebrows rose. "Something funny?"

"War paint?"

His gaze was blank for a moment before he realized she was talking about his face.

Laughing, he used the corner of his shirt to wipe the color away.

"Thank you for pointing that out to me. You could have just left me walking around town like that all day."

The mood had lightened so much Angelica wanted to burst out into a song of praise to God, but because she couldn't carry a tune to save her life, she prayed a silent thank-You instead.

Ever since coming back to Serendipity, she'd been on a roller coaster of ups and downs with Rowdy.

She much preferred the ups.

Because she still cared for Rowdy.

Knowing her feelings would show in her eyes, she quickly turned away, making a big deal of picking up Toby as if she'd heard him cry.

Her son was still sound asleep and hadn't made a peep. He was just an excuse for Angelica to keep her attention focused anywhere but at Rowdy.

After all that had happened between them, she hadn't considered that latent feelings for him might ramp up as suddenly and intensely as they had.

Of course, she would always care for him. She had once been ready to tie her life to his in marriage, as youthful and immature as that love might have been.

But this—*these* emotions were a whole other thing. In just a little over one short month, she had gotten to know Rowdy in ways she couldn't even have imagined in her youth.

She understood and truly appreciated the hard work that had turned him from a lanky boy to a well-muscled and weathered cowboy.

And most of all, she finally *got* the honor and integrity that made Rowdy rise far above all of the other men she'd ever known.

She would never share these newfound revelations with him. It was awkward enough to be around him, sometimes even painful, without blabbing out her emotional discovery.

Besides, he expected her to leave. To fulfill Granny's last wishes and then head on back to Denver, selling Granny's ranch to him.

And up until now, that's just what she'd intended to do. Or maybe she'd just blinded herself as to what was really going on in her heart.

"Is everything okay over there? How's Toby?" Rowdy called.

Heat flamed to her face and she kept her head bowed, carefully hiding it from Rowdy's gaze.

"I thought I heard something, but it's nothing."

Except it wasn't nothing.

Because what she'd heard was the call of her heart.

* * *

On the morning of the Fourth of July, Rowdy arrived at the public arena early to deliver the wild cows. He'd helped Ange load the sheep onto her trailer earlier, but she hadn't yet arrived and he was glad for a quiet moment to compose himself.

When the subject of the ranch rodeo had first come up at Cup O' Jo's, Rowdy had tried his best not to react.

In truth, every nerve ending in his body had snapped to life. Even the words *ranch rodeo* made him internally cringe as fear rumbled through his gut.

He'd avoided attending the annual ranch rodeo since the year he'd been injured, but if anyone had noticed, they'd been kind enough not to mention it.

But for some reason, he hadn't wanted Ange to know that the saddle bronc riding hadn't just injured his knee but had crushed his self-confidence, as well.

Pride, he supposed.

He'd been telling the truth when he'd told Ange that she hadn't forced him into the competition that fateful day. He wasn't a wrangler and he'd never started a horse in his life, but he could ride as well as the next cowboy, and anyway, it was a ranch rodeo. There were no rules about spurring and raking. All he had to do was somehow manage to stay in the saddle for eight seconds, any way he could.

How hard could that be?

As it turned out, he'd remained in the saddle for longer than eight seconds—or at least his foot had. His boot had caught in the stirrup and he couldn't get it loose. After the horse bashed his knee into the wall, causing him to lose his precarious balance, he'd been dragged along on the ground until he'd nearly passed out from the pain.

As far as he knew, his accident was the only major incident that had ever happened at the annual event, before or since, and it had been a freak accident that would never be repeated, so he shouldn't be worried. But this year it was teenagers competing in the games.

Nearly all of them had grown up doing a semblance of the kind of skills they'd be demonstrating today, but he couldn't help the hoof-in-the-gut feeling that came at odd intervals and caught him off-guard every time.

He didn't want Ange to see him this way. He didn't want *anyone* to see him like this, lacking the courage to face up to his fears. He'd better cowboy up, and quickly, because Ange's SUV and trailer were just now pulling into the arena.

He waved her over to where he was opening the tops of the paint buckets and stirring each color with a paint stick.

She placed Toby nearby, still strapped into his car seat, close enough to keep an eye on him but well away from the paint fumes.

"The teens are going to have a blast with this," she said, and then paused and observed him closely.

"Yeah. It'll be great fun," he agreed in a ridiculously and patently unbelievable tone that didn't belong to him at all. His voice hadn't been that high and squeaky since his own adolescence.

She put her hand on his forearm. Their gazes met and locked, her liquid blue eyes drawing him in. His heart pounded and his lungs forgot they were supposed to function on their own.

"Are you going to be okay?" she whispered. "Really?"

He wasn't even close to okay, except it had nothing to do with the ranch rodeo or saddle bronc riding and everything to do with the woman before him.

The empathy in her gaze nearly undid him, but there was something else in her eyes, and that was what caused his pulse to launch into the stratosphere.

It was more than her feeling sorry for him, more than the awful way they'd cast blame back and forth about something that was nobody's fault, or even all of the crazy mistakes they'd made between them.

She cared for him—as a woman cared for a man. He could see it. Feel the warmth emanating from her heart. And somewhere in this crazy storm of emotions stampeding through him, he realized that he cared for her, too.

Everything around them faded into the background, and all he could see was Ange, in all of her vibrant, colorful beauty, both inside and out.

Nothing else mattered besides the two of them, the man and the woman they had become.

Here.

Now.

The products of everything that had gone before, yes, but also with the potential of what was to come.

He framed her face with his palms and tipped her chin up with the pad of his thumb.

Then he paused, needing to be completely sure. If he was misreading the signals, if his heart was getting ahead of his head, the result could be disastrous.

"Rowdy." She said his name in her rich dark chocolate alto.

It was all the encouragement he needed, and he removed his hat and tossed it onto the ground. He brushed a long strand of her straight blond hair off her cheek and tucked it behind her ear, all without losing eye contact with her.

Slowly, his mouth came down on hers, starting with just the gentlest brush of his lips over hers before he kissed her in earnest.

Her lips were as soft and sweet as he remembered, but she had changed since the last time they had kissed, and so their kiss had changed, as well.

Different.

Mature.

Better.

Even though he'd been trying his hardest to keep them at bay, he recognized the emotions he was feeling—that they were sharing.

Rowdy closed his eyes and deepened the kiss, shoving his thoughts aside to make room for his heart to take over.

Chapter Ten

Ange ran her palms up Rowdy's chest and over his shoulders before locking her arms around his neck and pulling him closer.

He'd changed a lot from when they were young. He carried so much more strength and confidence in his frame. And while their kiss felt familiar, it was equally as foreign, and she desperately wanted to explore all that was new.

With Rowdy, she had always felt loved and cherished, but now she had a new appreciation for what was happening between them.

Something fresh.

Something wonderful.

And, perhaps, something that would last this time.

Even after he brushed one last kiss over her lips, he didn't let her go.

Their connection was magnetic as he tucked her close to his chest. She laid a hand over his heart, finding both comfort and exhilaration in how fast it pounded and how quickly his breath was coming.

"Ange," he murmured into her hair, his voice tender. "I don't—"

Whatever he'd been going to say was cut off by a bubbly laugh coming from the announcer's booth.

With the microphone *on*.

"Do you still think Frances made a mistake?" Jo asked with a throaty cackle. Her laugh reverberated through the thankfully still-empty arena. "Seems to me she knew *exactly* what she was doing."

Angelica expected Rowdy to immediately drop his hands from her waist and step away. When he didn't, Angelica took it upon herself to twist out of his arms.

As usual, she hadn't thought her action all the way through to its logical conclusion.

The moment she'd stepped into Rowdy's embrace, all she could do was follow her feelings and never mind her brain telling her to pump the brakes.

Now her emotions had left Rowdy exposed to ridicule. Angelica had no doubt Jo would razz the both of them. She had set herself up as some sort of errant matchmaker, and that was bad enough.

But what if someone else had come in and seen them kissing—one of the local ranchers or the teenagers who'd be competing in the day's events?

Was it a mistake to have followed her heart?

Her gaze tried to capture Rowdy's. Would he engage with Jo and her teasing, or shut her out with some inane explanation that she hadn't actually seen what she'd thought she saw?

He did neither.

He had already turned away and was opening the trailer door to lead the two wild cows to their pens.

As if their kiss had never happened.

Angelica could take a hint.

She could follow his lead.

"Where's Frank?" she called as she picked up Toby, still covered and in his car seat. She made a show of walking around and blatantly surveying the colored chalk lines that would be used in rounding up strays.

"Draggin' his feet and bellowin' up a fuss, as usual, the old goat. He'll get here when he gets here."

As the teenage competitors and the wranglers from the ranches they represented started arriving and unloading their horses and equipment, Angelica continued her last-minute check of the arena.

Anything to keep her mind off what had happened between her and Rowdy.

Had he just been caught up in the moment, or had he felt the same familiar-yet-different spark that she had?

She ended up at the pen holding the sheep she and Rowdy had brought from her ranch. Rowdy liked to tease her about it, but she recognized many of them now, and they each had a name. Every one of her sheep was an individual to her, not just part of a collective.

If saddle bronc riding was the most high-adrenaline, super-exciting event in the lineup, then mutton busting was the cutest, with the younger members of ranching families wearing hard helmets and getting plopped on top of a sheep to hold on for as long as they could.

Every one of those children would earn bragging rights today. They were the future of ranching.

However, this year, a new event might surpass even mutton busting for the cuteness factor. If the mutton busters were the future of ranching, then the Baby Cowboy was the future's future.

Angelica couldn't wait for Rowdy to see Toby's costume, but she was trying to keep it a secret until the actual unveiling happened.

She'd spent a lot of time planning and executing Toby's outfit, and he was absolutely adorable, if she did say so herself.

Which she did, even if she was totally biased.

First, she'd visited the tiny clothing section of Emerson's Hardware and cobbled together an outfit from what she was able to purchase and what she had on hand.

She'd never learned how to sew, so she thought the fact that she'd cut here and sewn there was pretty impressive, and she was proud of herself. Even if Toby didn't win the contest, he was and always would be number one in her heart.

As the stadium filled, Angelica looked around for Rowdy and found him leaning against the back side of one of the bronc riding chutes, his forearms on the fence and one boot propped on the bottom rung.

His gaze was distant, and she wondered if he was reliving the accident in his mind.

How could he not be?

She wandered over to where he was and bumped his shoulder with hers.

"Hey," she whispered.

"Hey." His voice had the texture of gravel, and when he glanced her direction, his eyes were glazed.

Angelica had removed the receiving blanket that she'd had tented over Toby's car seat and had artfully wrapped it around him so his costume was still hidden.

Rowdy's gaze dropped to Toby. He was awake and alert and immediately grabbed on to Rowdy's finger when he offered it.

"I'm really proud of you for staying and helping out the teenagers, and for getting out in the arena again," she said. "You once told me sometimes the best way to go beyond fear is to go through it. Today is that day for you, Rowdy."

His brow rose and his expression changed, although she couldn't quite discern what it meant.

"What?"

His lips curved up the slightest bit.

"I appreciate the encouragement. But would you believe I wasn't thinking about my accident?"

"No?"

He shook his head. "At least, not in the way I had expected to be haunted by it."

"It can't be easy for you to be here."

"No. It's not. And I'm not sure how I'm going to feel when the saddle bronc riding starts. But just now, I was thinking about *you*."

"Me?"

Yes, they'd shared that amazing kiss earlier, a real game changer as far as Angelica was concerned, but Rowdy had so much more to be thinking about right now. His past was going to rise up to meet him in a major way in just a couple of hours.

"I was thinking about how things might have been different if either one of us had reached out to the other. If we'd supported each other better. It's amazing to me how easily a simple miscommunication broke our relationship. If I hadn't been so caught up in my own issues, I would have been able to see what I was doing to you."

Angelica's throat tightened and tears burned in the back of her eyes.

"We both made mistakes," she said. "In my view,

mine were far worse than yours. But we can't go back, and I wouldn't want to. I might have had a miserable eight years away from Serendipity, but now I have Toby and I wouldn't change that for all the world."

Rowdy wiggled the finger Toby was grasping and the baby smiled, his eyes crinkling.

A low rumble came from Rowdy's chest. "Now tell me that wasn't a real smile."

"He always responds to you in a special way, perking up when he hears your voice, smiling when he sees your face."

"Really?" Rowdy's face colored and he stood an inch taller, looking very pleased with himself. And Toby.

Then he looked back at Toby and cleared his throat, his Adam's apple bobbing.

"I know the past is—what it is—but do you think maybe that we could work toward building something new for the future?"

Angelica's heart warmed until she was beaming with sunshine from the inside out.

Rowdy wasn't being unrealistic or suggesting they just try to pick up where they had left off all those years ago. That would be impossible anyway, because Toby was now in the picture.

But maybe, if they took it slow, they could start to build something new. Something better and more mature.

"We aren't the same people we were eight years ago," she started to say, meaning to agree with him, to let him know the tentative feelings he had expressed were reciprocated, that she was more than willing to take the next step, to explore what might be and not just what had been.

But just then, the microphone pitched in high, squeaky feedback that made Angelica and Rowdy flinch and Toby start crying.

"Sorry, folks," Jo said. "Just a small technical difficulty."

"His poor little ears," Angelica said, cringing.

"Don't worry, little dude. You'll be okay." He pressed a kiss to Toby's forehead and brushed a palm over his white-blond hair.

Angelica couldn't keep her eyes off Rowdy, and her heart was skipping beats all over the place.

He was so good with Toby.

He was so good to *her.*

"Toby's going to rock the Baby Cowboy contest," he said.

Angelica chuckled. "You haven't even seen his outfit yet."

Rowdy shrugged. "I don't need to. Your son is the cutest baby in Serendipity, bar none."

"Thank you for that," she said, a little choked up.

"Just telling it like it is."

Her heart swelled.

"I promise I'll be watching you and rooting for you during the saddle bronc riding."

"You know I'm just a pickup man, out there for safety's sake and not actually bronc riding, right?"

"I know. I just wish I could be out there with you." It was a silly thing for her to say. She'd be useless both to Rowdy and the kids riding the broncs. She just wanted to do something to prove she was ready to pursue a relationship with him. Be the partner she hadn't been before.

But Rowdy evidently didn't read between the lines,

or else he'd turned his focus completely on the rodeo to come.

"No worries, Ange. I will be just fine without you."

Rowdy's words had a double meaning. It was true that he had every faith he and his stocky black quarter horse gelding Hercules would be able to keep the bronc riding kids from being injured.

But he was also telling Ange that she didn't need to finish her statement.

What she *had* said was more than enough for him to catch the full drift of her meaning.

They were two completely different people now, not the young adults who'd believed in the kind of love that was only in movies, not real life.

Perhaps their kiss had been some kind of test for her, the opportunity to see if there was anything left of what love there had once been between them.

Rowdy felt sick to his stomach as he mounted Hercules and directed the teenagers into their first event, wild cow milking, a hilarious spectacle meant to get the crowd stoked up for the rest of the rodeo.

Why had he kissed her? He should have realized that he was moving too fast, in the wrong place at the wrong time.

Real romantic, Masterson. Way to blow it.

Kissing her in the middle of the rodeo arena right before a major town event, where anyone could have shown up. Thankfully, it had only been Jo, but that was bad enough.

Oh, Granny Frances, I wish you were here to help me sort this out. Was this what you wanted for us? Have I really messed it up?

Jo and Frank were keeping the events moving, and Rowdy had no choice but to turn his attention to the ranch rodeo. The teenagers "branded" cows with paint, showed their prowess at gathering strays and loaded and unloaded horse trailers with barely started horses, sometimes requiring quite a bit of pushing and pulling of both heads and hindquarters.

The noisy crowd was having a blast, cheering on the contestants and laughing up a storm, encouraging the teenagers to do their best.

Mutton busting in particular was a town favorite, with five-to-seven-year-olds, absolutely adorable little cowboys and cowgirls in hard helmets, holding on for dear life on a sheep which, unused to having a person on its back, bolted forward pell-mell.

And then, at last, came the new event, the one he and Ange had added to the lineup specifically for Toby and the one event Rowdy was actually looking *forward* to today.

"It's time for all our Baby Cowboys and Cowgirls to make their way to the front of the arena," Jo announced.

As usual, Jo was ready for the new event, wearing one of her infamous homemade T-shirts. This one read Let's Go, Babies! Which pretty much summed up her feelings on the new event, and apparently, her opinion on what was going to be the highlight of the rodeo.

Rowdy's pulse jumped, thundering as loudly as if he had his own baby in the race.

In a way, he guessed he did. Although he couldn't have explained why, he couldn't feel more emotionally bonded to Toby than if he was his own son.

Maybe it had something to do with how Rowdy was, and always had been, bonded to the baby's mother.

Whatever the cause, Rowdy's heart was thundering when it was time for Toby to make his official Serendipity debut.

Let's Go, Toby.

Chapter Eleven

A dozen mothers and fathers, all decked out in their country best, stood in the arena just before the announcer's platform holding their little stars in their arms for everyone to see.

Babies and toddlers from newborn to age two had been invited to participate, and Angelica was thrilled at the first year's turnout. She suspected this was going to be a new annual event and something the folks in town would look forward to.

Angelica and Toby were in the middle of the row. Not first, not last. She just hoped the focus would be on Toby and not on herself.

At Jo's announcement, parents unwrapped their children from the blankets covering them and revealed adorable cowboy and cowgirl costumes to the cheering audience.

One at a time, each mother and father walked around the perimeter of the arena so everyone could get a good look at the babies. Angelica didn't miss the fact that she was the only single parent in the group, but it was what it was.

Her life belonged to Toby, and that was good enough for her.

It had to be.

The costumes ran from quickly thrown together to more intricate, although nothing near what Angelica had done with Toby. She suspected that most parents were counting on the cuteness factor for *their* baby to win the contest.

And there was some truth to that. In the parents' eyes, their babies were the cutest.

And it hadn't been a stretch for most of the families to come up with Western outfits. Most of the toddlers already owned at least one pair of denim jeans and a tiny pair of cowboy boots or mud boots. Some even had hats in toddler sizes. Kids started learning how to do ranch chores early in Serendipity, accompanying their parents from the time they could walk.

All of the babies were by far the cutest little ranchers she'd ever seen.

The smaller babies' outfits typically leaned another direction—onesies with cute country sayings on them. Some of the baby girls had bows in their hair, and there was one baby boy who was dressed in nothing more than a denim-decorated diaper.

Every one of them was adorable, too.

But then again, so was Toby. And she'd put a lot of thought and effort into his wardrobe. Maybe it was because she'd been the one to think up this extra event, or maybe it was that she was newly returned to the country, but she had been more detailed in planning Toby's costume. She'd tried to see the big picture and not just focus on a particular item of clothing.

He was a chunky monkey and had been able to fit

into toddler blue jeans, with some minor modifications in length and girth. She'd purchased the smallest bright-blue-checked chambray shirt and used safety pins to size it to Toby.

She'd even taken a length of black ribbon to make a belt and had formed a shiny belt buckle out of tin foil, on which she'd glitter-glued the word *COWBOY*. But her pièce de résistance was the cotton-ball sheep with a black eye and red smile that she'd pinned to his shirt.

As a final touch, she'd found a small length of rope that someone had abandoned in a ditch near her ranch. She'd washed it clean and looped it into a lasso, which she pressed into his fist when it was time for them to make their promenade around the arena.

She'd walked about three feet when a shadow fell over her and she realized someone was walking alongside her.

She looked up to see a grinning Rowdy, waving at the crowd and encouraging them to cheer even louder.

"Rowdy," she exclaimed, before lowering her voice. "What are you doing?"

"When you unveiled Toby's outfit, I just knew I had to be there with you guys. I'm proud of my little cowboy. But the sheep on his shirt? Now that's ingenious."

She flashed him a questioning look.

"I know. It doesn't make any sense. But we sheep farmers have to stick together."

Which made sense, she supposed, and it was a nice thing for him to say. She was shocked that Rowdy had joined them, but mostly, she was grateful.

She'd seen how Rowdy had bonded with Toby. With her *prodigal daughter* reputation, Toby was at a natural disadvantage straight out of the gate. Rowdy's presence with them evened out the scales.

If he could get over their negative history together, surely members of the community could overlook her past and possibly allow her to find her future here.

When they returned to their spot in front of the podium and Rowdy propped his cowboy hat on Toby's head, there was no question as to which baby had most captured the audience's hearts. The crowd was roaring for the baby with the glitzy belt buckle.

For once, she had done something right.

"Ladies and gentlemen," Jo announced, her voice crackling over the microphone's feedback. "We've had our share of cute and lots of laughs. Now it's time for a shot of pure adrenaline in our last event and a fan favorite, saddle bronc riding!"

Rowdy shifted in the saddle, his attention glued to the first chute, where a dark-haired girl wearing a white straw cowboy hat was making last-minute adjustments to her balance on the bronc.

"Let's give it up for Erin Smith riding Charlie Horse."

The crowd cheered. Rowdy tensed and his stockiest quarter horse, Hercules, skittered to the side, reacting to his negative energy.

Erin nodded and a ranch hand pulled the chute gate open.

Charlie Horse sprang into action, twisted and turned; his back legs kicked out and his front legs bucked, sometimes at the same time.

Rowdy pressed his knees into Hercules as he laser focused on Erin and Charlie. Mostly his eyes were glued to the horse, watching for signs that he would make a sudden unexpected move, but from time to time Rowdy glanced up to see how Erin was faring.

If her expression was anything to go by, she was reveling in the ride, totally in control, solid in the saddle and calling to Charlie to urge him onto the best ride she could have.

Eight seconds seemed to take forever to Rowdy, who was counting down in milliseconds, but Erin easily rode out her time and dismounted on her own without Rowdy coming alongside her.

He grabbed Charlie's flank strap and the horse immediately calmed down, happy to be herded off the arena grounds.

Rowdy swallowed hard. One down, four to go, and then he would be able to breathe again.

Next up was a much smaller boy named Ryan who didn't look to be as old as his peers. Maybe he was a late bloomer. Rowdy was worried that he wouldn't be able to handle the horse he'd drawn, but another eight seconds went by without incident. The little scrapper held on like a trooper, and though he flipped and flopped a bit, he stayed in the saddle.

Third up was another girl, Jessie, riding a horse named Cricket. Odd name for a ranch horse, Rowdy thought, but he made a decent bronc. Jessie also stayed on the eight seconds and made a smooth dismount with Rowdy's help.

The fourth horse, Rocket, was ridden by a boy named Philip. Unfortunately for Philip, Rocket didn't feel like living up to his name for the event. He barely bucked at all, just throwing his back feet out from time to time as if the flank strap merely annoyed him.

So it was a disappointed boy who ended his eight

seconds with Rocket. The horses' movements made up half of the score, with the cowboy's or cowgirl's riding making up the other half. The rules stated that if a cowboy or cowgirl pulled a horse that didn't live up to the half of the score required for the horse, he or she could choose to make a second ride on another horse. But since it was a ranch rodeo and there were no cash or trophies awarded, Rowdy doubted Philip would bother.

The fifth and last teenage cowboy to make his saddle bronc ride was Jace on a horse called Crash. Hercules shifted, alerting Rowdy to the fact that he'd tensed up again. There was no reason to believe the horse was named on his behavior, but Rowdy wouldn't rest easy until the ride was finished.

Crash was a decent bronc, but as with the other teenaged bronc riders, Jace had spent his life on the ranch and bronc riding came naturally to him.

Rowdy's adrenaline sparked at about six seconds in, when Crash went one way and Jace went the other. There was nowhere for that kid to go but down, but at least the horse had tossed him into the middle of the arena.

Thankfully, Jace landed on the padding the good Lord had given him and immediately rolled to his feet, stalked the few yards to grab his brown cowboy hat off the dirt where it had landed and waved it to the riser full of friends and neighbors to let them know he hadn't been hurt. Everyone cheered for him as loudly as they had the others, and he walked out of the arena with a smile on his face.

Rowdy was about to rein Hercules out of the arena so he could go find Ange and they could celebrate their success with the ranch rodeo when the microphone crackled again.

"Don't leave your seats just yet, folks. Rocket wasn't much of a bronc today, and Philip was unable to show off his bronc riding skills, so he has elected to take a second ride, this time on a horse named Shy Boy."

Rowdy groaned.

Couldn't they just be done already?

Hopefully Shy Boy's name *was* indicative of his personality and they could get these eight seconds over with.

Rowdy was *so* done with this ranch rodeo. He wanted to spend the rest of the day out on the neighborhood green, picnicking with Ange and Toby, enjoying the games and fireworks and showing off to friends and neighbors their adorable little winner of the Baby Cowboy contest.

It was high time for the townsfolk to get over what had happened in the past between Ange and Rowdy. After what they'd shared earlier today, opening their hearts to each other, he hoped he could convince her to stay in town long enough for them to truly pursue their relationship.

His attention had been distracted just for that one moment, as he was considering the future, when Philip nodded and Shy Boy sprang into the arena, furiously bucking and kicking and turning in tight circles, determined to get the flank strap off at any cost, never mind the rider on his back.

For the first couple of seconds, Philip looked as if he was off-balance and Rowdy thought he'd probably hit the dirt pretty quickly and end the ride, but then Philip somehow shifted and regained control.

But Shy Boy was having none of it.

One second the horse was in the middle of the arena as he twisted and turned and altogether put on a good show for the spectators, who were yelling and hooting and cheering him on.

The next moment, the crowd went dead silent as Shy Boy charged straight toward the wall.

Rowdy didn't think. He just acted, pressing his heels into Hercules's side and leaning forward, giving Hercules his full head.

Hercules launched into a gallop, sensing his rider's inner torment.

Rowdy's first thought had been to try to herd Shy Boy away from the wall, but he immediately realized that wasn't going to happen.

Shy Boy was going too fast and was too panicked to realize what he was doing. The whites of his eyes were showing and his ears were pinned back as he whipped his head from side to side in a frantic attempt to lose the rider.

Philip was yelling for Shy Boy to stop and clinging on to the saddle for dear life, with one hand twisted into Shy Boy's mane.

But despite everything, Shy Boy put his head down and made straight for the arena wall.

"Jump off," Rowdy hollered. "Philip, jump off."

But Philip either didn't hear or couldn't move. He appeared every bit as spooked as his horse and only clung tighter as Shy Boy continued galloping forward.

Rowdy reined Hercules between Shy Boy and the wall. He had purposefully picked Hercules because of his size and speed, but he could never have imagined that the scene would play out before him the way it did.

All he knew was that he had to slip into the space between Shy Boy and the arena wall.

As the air created by Hercules's gallop drove the hat off Rowdy's head, Rowdy gritted his teeth and prayed that God would keep Philip safe. Hercules safe. Shy Boy.

And him.

A moment later, Shy Boy lit into Hercules's side and both horses reared and made course corrections—Shy Boy to the middle of the arena and Rowdy into the wall, where his entire left side, head to toe, collided with the concrete.

Pain detonated in Rowdy's knee, and his head exploded with fireworks as bright as the ones Serendipity planned for this evening.

Rowdy had picked Hercules in the hope that the larger, stronger horse would help keep the teenagers' horses under control, and he had.

But at what price?

Rowdy's gaze was clouding in pain.

Something was off.

He felt as if he was seeing everything at a great distance, and then his vision blurred and doubled and he tried to blink it back into focus.

He was mindful enough to pull his boots from the stirrups so he wouldn't be dragged around the arena as he had been last time he'd found himself in this position. With his strength greatly failing, he gripped at his saddle horn and plunged one hand into Hercules's mane. The horse slowed, but it wasn't enough for Rowdy to stay in the saddle.

He was going to go down.

His left leg would give out on him the moment he

hit the turf and his vision was already gray, but he did everything he could to remain on Hercules for as long as possible.

Before his body gave out, he had to see what was happening with Philip and Shy Boy.

Had he saved them?

Gritting his teeth, he narrowed his gaze on Philip, trying to focus through his double vision and the darkness threatening to overcome him.

He watched as Philip slid safely from Shy Boy and ran toward the arena gate while one of the mounted ranch hands released the flank strap from Shy Boy.

Rowdy had done it.

Philip was safe.

His last thought before slumping over the neck of Hercules and giving in to the darkness was of Ange and Toby.

He hadn't been able to express how he really felt.

Now the game had changed once again.

She might never know that he was in love with her.

Chapter Twelve

❧

"N-o-o-o-o!" Angelica screamed as Rowdy's limp body rolled over Hercules's neck and he slammed to the ground, flat on his back.

"Please, God, let him be okay." She was praying aloud and she didn't care who heard her.

She grabbed Toby, in his car seat, and dashed out of the announcer's booth and onto the arena floor, where Rowdy was surrounded by the ranch hands, who had been pickup men like Rowdy, one on his horse and two on the arena floor, crouched around Rowdy's unmoving form.

Paramedics were on hand and were also running toward Rowdy with their equipment and a stretcher. Angelica wanted to be right beside him, but there were too many people already there and the paramedics needed room to do their work.

Her heart hammered as her gaze took Rowdy in.

His left leg was bent at an odd angle and a large purple bruise and enormous goose egg was already coloring his forehead.

Oh, Lord. Please no.

Was he breathing?

She couldn't tell.

His chest wasn't visibly rising and falling, as it should have been after surviving such a fall.

She wanted to be beside him, to hold him in her arms and tell him all the secrets of her heart that she had tried to hold back.

Oh, why hadn't she just been honest and told him how much she loved him?

Now he might never know.

Jo reached her and restrained her from moving to Rowdy's side with a firm, no-nonsense hug around her shoulders that Angelica, feeling as weak as she ever had in her life, could not break.

Who knew that the old woman was so strong?

"You have to let the paramedics do their job, honey," Jo coaxed. "I know you want to be at Rowdy's side, but right now what he needs is medical help. And our prayers."

Angelica knew Jo was right, but her heart was shattering into pieces as she watched the paramedics kneel before Rowdy and assess his injuries.

"He's not breathing," she sobbed. "Do something!"

Why weren't the paramedics doing CPR?

"He's just had the wind knocked out of him," Frank Spencer said, arriving at his wife's side and awkwardly patting Angelica's shoulder. "He landed flat on his back."

Angelica's tears poured and her breath came in tiny bursts of hiccups. She was hyperventilating, but she couldn't control her breathing as she watched the paramedics put an oxygen mask over Rowdy's mouth and a neck brace to guard against spinal injuries.

What if this accident was worse than the last one? What if Rowdy was paralyzed? He was a fighter, but he was also a rancher. Taking his life's work away from him would kill his spirit.

After the paramedics had stabilized his breathing and his neck, they carefully rolled him onto a back-board and stretcher. Angelica followed them to the ambulance, feeling entirely helpless as they loaded him up and headed off down the road.

"What about his knee?" she asked to no one in particular, her voice nothing more than a dry croak.

"They've stabilized him, which is the most important part," Jo said. "And now they want to get him to the hospital as soon as possible. I'm sure they'll splint his leg on the way."

"The hospital is nearly an hour away. Shouldn't they have their lights and sirens on? Or be using a helicopter?"

"It's their call, sweetie. If the paramedics thought this was a life-or-death situation, you'd better believe they would have called a helicopter to transport him. If they think he can travel in an ambulance, especially without hitting their lights, that's a good thing, right? It means he's stable enough for them to continue care on the way."

"I need to be there with him."

Jo didn't appear surprised at all by her admission.

"Of course you do. What do we need to do to make that happen?"

Toby kicked off his blanket in a not-so-subtle reminder that Angelica had other responsibilities than just Rowdy. She couldn't leave Toby and run off to be with Rowdy, no matter how much she ached to be by his side.

"Toby will have to go with us, as well, of course," Jo said, as if reading her mind. "I'll tell you what. How about if Frank and I rent a couple of rooms at the hotel next door to the hospital—one for us and one for you and Toby. That way I can babysit Toby while you are visiting with Rowdy, but you won't be too far away from your son."

Tears burned her eyes so that she could barely see Jo through the moisture.

"I couldn't ask you to do that."

"Did you hear anybody asking? You just let old Jo take care of everything, okay?"

Angelica felt like she was not all there. Her mind was in a haze and her heart was with Rowdy. She wouldn't have been able to work this out on her own, and was more grateful to Jo than she could have ever expressed.

Barely aware of the crowd of people exiting the bleachers, Angelica allowed Jo to lead her to a place to sit down, then Jo pulled out her cell phone, promising she wouldn't be more than a moment.

"On hold," she told Angelica after she'd dialed. She shook her head and her red curls bobbed. Covering the receiver, she nodded toward her husband. "Frank, honey, pull the truck around."

"Already going," he assured her.

"Yes, hello," Jo said as someone picked up on the other end of the line. "I'm going to need two rooms for an indeterminate amount of time. Please make them adjacent, if possible. We've got someone in the hospital and it will help us tremendously if we can be next to each other. Oh—and can you please add a crib to one of the rooms?"

She nodded. "Good. Fantastic. We will be checking in in a couple of hours. Put everything in my name."

As Jo continued to give the hotel her information, Angelica fed Toby a bottle of formula and tried to pull herself together. She would be no good to Rowdy if she was a blubbering mess, and Toby was picking up on her distress.

She needed to be strong for both their sakes.

Waiting for Jo to finish and Frank to pull around, she watched a couple of Rowdy's friends loading her sheep into a trailer.

"Those are mine," she said as Jo ended her call.

"They know, honey. You and Rowdy planned this gig, but there were more than just the two of you involved in the execution."

"There were?" Angelica wondered why she hadn't noticed. Maybe because she'd been too wrapped up in Rowdy.

"Yes. Don't worry. They'll deliver your sheep back to your property."

"All of my sheep," she squeaked. "And Rowdy's. What am I going to do? I can't just leave. The ranches don't run themselves."

"That's what friends are for," Jo affirmed.

"But I don't have any friends."

Jo shook her head. "I don't think that's true. Maybe when you first came back to town, it might have been. But people have been watching you with Toby. And with Rowdy. They've seen you in church. They may not know quite how to approach you without bringing up your past, but trust me when I tell you they will have your back during this tribulation. That's just how the folks in Serendipity are."

Angelica fought the sobs that threatened to erupt. She simply could not keep crying every time something happened to her, bad or good, or she wouldn't be able to get through this.

Rowdy needed her to be strong.

So did Toby.

No matter how she felt inside, no matter how her stomach churned and her heart ached and worry clouded her mind like a thunderstorm, she had to be strong.

And she would be.

Rowdy groaned. His eyelids felt like hundred-pound weights had been placed on each of them and he couldn't force them open no matter how hard he tried.

Every muscle in his body ached, even ones he hadn't known he had. He focused his mind on attempting to move, but nothing seemed to work. When he finally got his left fingers to wiggle, they sent a shot of white-hot pain up his arm.

Where was he?

He could hear a steady beeping from some kind of machine to the left of him, but not much else. He knew he was in bed, but for some reason he felt pinned down, as if someone had taken away his ability to control his own body.

And there was something else—something so quiet it took a moment for him to identify what it was.

Breathing.

Soft, steady breathing.

As his eyes slowly opened, he blinked heavily to focus his gaze. He tried to lift his head, but a gentle hand on his shoulder eased him back down.

"Take it easy, son. Try not to move."

He knew that voice.

Jo Spencer.

Why would Jo Spencer be…?

Suddenly it all came back to him in a horrifying rush that made him so lightheaded he nearly passed out again.

Shy Boy heading for the wall with a terrified Philip on his back.

Rowdy urging Hercules between them.

And then—nothing.

"H-hospital?" he asked through dry lips.

"That's right." Jo brushed a sliver of ice over his lips and then gently slid it into his mouth. "We're at Mercy Medical Center in San Antonio. You were taken here yesterday by ambulance from the ranch rodeo. You've been pretty out of it since then."

He groaned.

"You've had surgery on your knee and they set your left wrist in a cast. You've got a big ol' purple goose egg on your forehead. Thankfully, you have a hard head." Jo chuckled at her own joke.

"Water?"

With Jo supporting his neck, he lifted his head just enough to be able to take a sip of lukewarm water out of a straw.

It was only then that he realized someone else was in the room with him.

The breathing he'd heard.

It hadn't been Jo.

Ange had dragged a chair to his bedside and had crooked her elbow on the side of his mattress. She was sound asleep with her head in her palm.

Jo chuckled. "That woman won't leave your side.

Hasn't budged since the moment we got here. She would have been in surgery with you if they would have let her. As it is, I've been bringing Toby to her here at the hospital so she doesn't have to leave you alone."

"She doesn't need to do that."

Ange had to be really exhausted. She was still slumped in a dead sleep with her head in her hand, despite Rowdy and Jo having a conversation. That couldn't be comfortable.

He felt guilty that she'd refused to leave even to take care of Toby or get a good night's sleep, but at the same time his heart welled with the thought that she cared enough to stay with him.

Rowdy's right hand was near enough to her arm that he was able, with effort, to stretch his arm out to touch her elbow.

She jumped up as if she'd been zapped with a bolt of electricity.

"What?" she asked, coming immediately alert. "What's wrong?"

Rowdy tried to chuckle, but it sounded like tires on gravel through his dry throat.

"Rowdy." The sound of his name in her rich alto warmed his chest like a cup of hot chocolate on a snowy day. "Are you hurting? Should I get a nurse?"

He chuckled, then cringed at the rippling effect of his sore muscles on his extremities—especially his left wrist and his knee.

He was in pain, all right, but he didn't want Ange to call a nurse. Not just yet.

"What happened at the ranch rodeo?" he croaked.

Jo patted his shoulder and then gave Ange an animated hug.

"I'll just leave the two of you alone for a minute while I check on Toby. His honorary uncle Frank is entertaining him at the moment with his gruffy, growly faces, but I'll bet that sweet baby is ready to be loved on some by Auntie Jo."

"Thanks," Ange said, her voice cracking with emotion.

With a sigh, she straightened her chair and sat down, pulling her knees up and circling them with her arms.

"What's that face for?" he asked, trying to smile for her sake but not sure he got much past a grimace.

She shook her head and tears filled her eyes, but she didn't speak.

Wow. Did he really look all that bad?

He felt awful, but now it was as much because she was distressed and his heart was hurting for her as that he'd clearly sustained some injuries in the ranch rodeo.

"Hey, do you think you could hitch this bed up for me so I can sit up?"

She rose the head of the bed enough for him to view the damage and take stock of why his pain was a six out of ten on the pain scale.

His left knee was in a brace. That bit of news didn't surprise him, but he felt a little discouraged by it. He'd recovered from a knee injury before, and no matter how long it took and how hard he would have to work, he would recover again.

His chest was tightly wrapped and he suspected he might have bruised a rib or two. And as Jo had said, his left wrist was in a cast.

"Well, I can see that my left side took the brunt of whatever happened to me," he said, and then paused, hoping to encourage her to fill in the blanks.

She just stared at him, her bottom lip caught between her teeth.

"I remember Philip rocking out on Shy Boy, and I remember thinking he was going to hit the wall. He didn't, did he?"

Ange shook her head. "No. When you and Hercules charged in, Shy Boy veered off. Philip was able to dismount without hurting himself, thankfully."

"That's good."

"You're a hero. Everybody thinks so." She reached out and touched his forearm and he slid his hand down to thread his fingers with hers.

"I don't care what everybody thinks, Ange. It only matters to me what you think."

"I think what you did was amazing. And selfless."

He still couldn't remember every detail about what had happened during the ranch rodeo, but anything that garnered that adoration in Ange's eyes and that kind of praise from her lips had been worth it, fractured bones and all.

Because he felt the same way.

He was in love with her.

And he wanted to be her hero.

His heart swelled to bursting as he struggled to find the words to tell her how much he wanted her and Toby in his life, but his mouth was as dry as desert sand and try as he might his emotions remained unspoken.

Could she read his feelings in his eyes?

For a moment, their gazes met and held and he thought he saw a glimpse of his emotions mirrored in her eyes before her gaze flashed with something else.

Doubt? Uncertainty?

She stood and slipped her hand out of his, brushing

the tears from her cheeks before she turned her back on him and went to look out the window.

It took her a moment to gather her thoughts before she turned back to him and spoke with a low, gritty determination.

"And once again, after I encouraged you to ride, you're in a hospital with multiple injuries. How long do you think it will take you to recover and walk again this time?"

He tried to straighten his shoulders but his bruised ribs complained.

"I don't know," he said honestly. He hadn't even talked to the doctor yet and his head was swimming with pain. "It doesn't matter." With Ange by his side, he felt as if he could conquer anything. His new physical issues were just another hurdle to overcome.

"But it does," she whispered raggedly. "It proves what I've been saying all along. You should never have trusted me. Even when I think I'm doing the right thing for you, that I'm supporting you, I make the wrong decision and you get hurt. How many times does this have to happen before you realize how bad I am for you?"

He gritted his teeth to speak through the pain. "I thought we worked all that out."

"So did I." Her voice cracked. "But I was wrong. I want you to be happy, Rowdy."

"I am happy—when I'm with you and Toby."

Emotional pain crossed her gaze that rivaled anything Rowdy was feeling physically. "I'm surprised you can say that in your present condition—in the hospital with the kind of injuries you sustained."

"Which has zero—do you hear me, Ange, *zero*—to

do with what you may or may not have said to me. It was my idea to ride pickup, not yours."

"But I encouraged you."

"You did. And you know what? That meant more to me than you'll ever know. This injury," he said, jerking his head toward his left side, "is nothing compared to that. I'm not sure I could have gotten out there if it wasn't for you."

"Which just goes to prove my point." She sniffed and pressed her palms to her eyes.

"No, it doesn't. I don't know how to make you understand. You helped me conquer a fear that had been hanging over my head for eight years."

"And in the process, you landed in the hospital."

"Yes. But not from doing something stupid. This time, I'm here because I saved a teenager from what might have been a bad accident. Big difference. And again, not your fault."

Her gaze met his. Did he see a flicker of hope in her eyes?

She blinked, and the spark was extinguished.

"Now the whole town knows you're a hero." Her low alto was rich with meaning.

"The only opinion I'm interested in is yours. Do *you* think I'm a hero, Ange?"

His breath caught in his throat while he waited for his words to sink in. For her to realize what he was really saying.

A knock at the door interrupted them before Ange could say another word.

A nurse came in to check his vitals and ask about his pain on the pain scale.

"It's not too bad," he said through gritted teeth, cringing when the nurse put her hand on his shoulder.

He wasn't fooling anyone.

But he didn't want to drift away, not when he was so close to making everything right in his world.

The nurse added pain medicine to his IV and his head immediately became fuzzy.

"Ange," he said, reaching for her with his right arm, desperate to finish the conversation.

She stepped forward and took his hand.

But before he could speak, another knock sounded and a man in light green scrubs came into the room.

"Sorry to interrupt you," the orderly said. "I'm here to take you down for an MRI."

First the pain medicine, and now this. Rowdy growled with frustration.

The orderly could not have interrupted at a worse time. Before Rowdy knew that Ange had understood his full meaning.

Understood that he loved her and Toby and wanted them to be together always.

His last thought as the orderly pushed him away and he gave himself in to the pain medication was of Ange and Toby, and the family he so desperately wanted them to be.

Chapter Thirteen

With tears in her eyes and her heart in pieces, Angelica packed up the last box, full of the items she would need immediately when she got to their new home, and marked it with a big red X so she would know to unpack it first.

That she didn't know exactly where that home would be was admittedly a problem, but if she had to, she and Toby could stay in a hotel for a couple of weeks while she searched for the perfect place.

It wouldn't be in downtown Denver. That was no longer her scene. Maybe something in the suburbs, where folks settled down and raised their families.

Lakewood, maybe. Or Westminster.

She was no closer to figuring out what she wanted to do with her life than the day she'd moved back to Serendipity. She'd been too caught up in running the ranch. But again, she could buy herself time by working another job for a paycheck—just not necessarily the one she would eventually make a career path of.

Watching Rowdy being wheeled away by the orderly was the most painful moment of her life, and she'd left the hospital soon after. Despite what he'd said, all the arguments he'd made in her defense, seeing him laid up in the hospital, and knowing that, in part at least, she was the one who put him there was more than her heart could handle.

She had encouraged him back into the arena. Granted, she hadn't realized he could get hurt as a pickup man almost as easily as he had on the bronc eight years ago, but she should have known that if he saw a teenager in danger he would put himself out to make sure nothing bad happened.

She sighed and brushed her hair away from her face with the palm of her hand. Angelica's time on Granny's ranch in Serendipity had taught her a lot. When she looked in the mirror, she saw a mature and determined woman looking back at her, a mother who could and would take care of herself and her son, something she hadn't been certain she would be able to do.

Her only regret was having to leave the Bar C behind.

And Rowdy.

But the time had come, because despite everything, despite knowing she would leave her heart behind with Rowdy she knew it was time for her to go.

She wanted to be the right woman for him, the one who, along with Toby, would become his family. Someone who could support him, walk beside him and be his partner in life.

Instead, she had floundered through her multiple attempts to be a rancher and by encouraging him to get back out in the rodeo arena had kicked the cane right out from underneath him.

How many times would he have to suffer because of her?

There was the ranch rodeo eight years ago, and then again last week. The Psycho Rooster, who had scratched him all up and had left what she was sure would become a scar on his jaw—and all because he was trying to protect her from her own foolishness.

She'd left him on the night of their wedding rehearsal and had broken his heart.

This time, when she left Serendipity this second— and last—time, she knew for sure that it was *her* heart that was once again breaking. Hopefully, Rowdy would realize she'd done him a favor, kept him from falling all over again.

As hard as it would be, she wouldn't leave without telling him goodbye this time, even though he already knew the reasons she had to go. She planned to visit the hospital later in the day and bring Toby along for their last farewell. She had learned that much from her past mistakes.

She taped up the box she'd been packing and moved it into the living room, stacking it on top of a couple of other similar-sized boxes.

There weren't many. She and Toby traveled light, and she hadn't purchased much. Other than what they'd brought with them, there were a few sentimental items of Granny's that she wanted to take, but nothing that took up much room.

A quilt. Granny's Bible. An old photograph of Granny and Gramps on the day they were married.

Her heart ached with longing. She could never settle for less than what Granny and Gramps had had, a marriage that withstood the test of time, up until the moment Granny lost Gramps to a sudden heart attack.

She would leave going through the rest of Granny's things to Jo, who would know better than she would how to deal with those items. Angelica had already had enough emotional overload to last her a lifetime. Sorting Granny's belongings would only give her more to grieve over.

She stooped and kissed Toby's forehead. Toby's gaze, far less hazy than when he was a newborn, fixed on her mouth. He lifted one fist to her lips and she gently kissed it. No matter what was right or wrong in her world, she had her son.

Three loud raps sounded on her front door, followed by two more, rousing her from her melancholy.

She wasn't expecting anyone. No one even knew she was leaving, and she wanted to keep it that way.

She hated goodbyes. She'd already informed Jo that she was leaving, and to her surprise, Jo hadn't argued. Maybe the old woman knew how hard this was for her. The only goodbye that still needed to be said would be handled later this afternoon.

Maybe Jo was here to make one last-ditch effort to change her mind about leaving.

"Who do you think that is, big guy?" she asked Toby in a singsong voice she wasn't feeling. She swung the door open, her gaze still on her son. "Are you expecting somebody?"

"Just you and Toby," a deep voice replied. "Why? Do you have someone else hiding in there?"

"Rowdy." Her heart jumped into her throat as he let himself in the door, stepping slowly and leaning heavily on his crutches. "When did you get out of the hospital? What are you doing here?"

Propping his crutches in front of him, he reached into the back pocket of his jeans and withdrew an envelope.

It was an achingly familiar sensation, reading *Angelica and Rowdy* scribbled on the outside in Granny's scratchy script.

She'd known there would be more letters, but she'd intended to leave before getting caught up in the next one. Rowdy needed to recuperate, not run all over town doing who knew what.

Attending picnics.

Feeding sheep.

Getting his bad knee smashed up saving a teenager at a ranch rodeo.

"Special delivery," he said with a grin. "They finally cut me loose from the hospital this afternoon. I thought I'd bring this letter out here in person so we can get right on it and solve our mystery once and for all."

"I don't think so, Rowdy." Her traitorous heart pounded so hard she thought perhaps Rowdy could hear it.

He frowned. "I don't get it. What's changed?"

"Me."

"But Granny—"

"Wouldn't want me to get in the way of you living your life to the fullest."

"What's that supposed to mean?"

"I called the local Realtor. He's going to get with my lawyer and work out the details of the sale of the ranch to you."

His jaw tightened. He looked like he was going to say something, but then he stopped and shook his head.

"No," he said at last, his tone brooking no argument.

"No?"

This was exactly why she'd been trying to leave town without a fuss. So that *this* didn't happen. She didn't know if her heart could handle it.

"Not without opening this envelope. Jo said it was the last one. I don't think you should make any permanent plans without finishing the course and fulfilling Granny Frances's last wishes, do you?"

She blew out an audible breath. That was precisely what she'd been about to do, but now that he was here, with the envelope in his palm, she supposed she might as well see this through. It wasn't as if he was going to let it go. And frankly, she wasn't strong enough to send him away.

She'd planned to say goodbye to him at the hospital. But since he was here, she might as well take advantage of his presence and part with him here in the privacy of her own home.

She picked up Toby from where he was cushioned in his bouncer and pulled him close to her shoulder, seeking comfort from the feel of him in her arms. His baby scent and the precious way he sucked on his fist always calmed her, even when she was as distressed as she was feeling right now.

"So open it." She turned away from Rowdy and paced to the other end of the room.

She heard him shake out the paper and clear his throat, then she turned back toward him just as he read the words.

"Find My Treasure."

"What do you think?" Rowdy asked, scratching his jaw. "Something buried in the back yard?"

She shook her head. "Too over-the-top, even for Granny. She would have kept her treasure close to her. In her personal space."

"Her bedroom?"

"If I had to guess."

"Haven't you been in there? Surely you would have noticed a treasure chest."

"I'm not sure we're looking for an actual chest, and I can't even speculate as to what Granny meant. But no, I haven't been in her bedroom. My grief is still too fresh and I couldn't hack going in there on my own. Seeing Granny's stuff. Being overwhelmed by memories."

Rowdy leaned forward on his crutches and reached for her hand and, Lord help her, she didn't pull it away.

"Happy memories, though, right?" he asked, a catch in his voice.

"Yes. So many."

"Me, too." He paused and squeezed her hand. "I think this is exactly what she wanted. For us to do this together. For me to be here with you. You can lean on me anytime you need to. You know that, don't you?"

Tears burned in the back of her eyes as she nodded fiercely.

She knew that, which was why leaving would be so hard.

"Well, maybe not physically lean on me," he joked, "or we both might tip over."

His words brought a soft smile to her lips despite the ache in her heart.

She leaned down and grabbed the baby bouncer and then gestured down the hall toward Granny's room. "Do you mind going in first?"

"Not at all."

She took a deep breath and followed him through the door into Granny's room.

"Whatever we find in here," he said, "we'll deal with together, okay?"

She nodded, unable to speak.

Angelica placed the bouncer on the floor next to Granny's bed and propped Toby in it.

"Where should we start?" he asked.

"I don't know. Where would you keep your treasure?"

"Assuming I had any? In the closet?"

"Works for me."

She had to remind herself to breathe as he set his crutches aside and dug into the closet. They sorted through Granny's clothing, pushing hangers aside so they could investigate the shelves in the back.

The whole closet smelled of Granny, the sweet scent of rose petals that Angelica would forever link with her.

She blinked away tears, but more took their place.

"I don't see anything that looks like a treasure chest," Rowdy said.

Angelica chuckled through her grief.

"Again, not necessarily a treasure chest," she reminded him.

"I know. But if anyone was going to keep their treasure in a chest, it would be Granny Frances, right?"

He was right about that.

But where else should they look?

Toby made a little mewling sound and Angelica glanced over to make sure he was doing well.

As usual, his fist was in his mouth and he was sucking loudly, but then she noticed he was clutching an old piece of ribbon.

"Where did you get that, little man? It probably shouldn't go into your mouth."

She reached out to take the ribbon away from him and realized it was attached to something, a longer ribbon disappearing under the corner of the bed.

"Rowdy?" she said, following the path of the ribbon until her hand closed around a box the size of a shoebox.

"Yeah?" he asked, popping his head out of the closet. He had left his hat on the hat rack at the front door as he always did, and his blond curls were ruffled with static cling from the clothes.

"I think Toby might have found something here."

As Rowdy sat on the edge of the bed, she pulled the box out from underneath it.

It was an old shoe box, decorated with ribbons that were probably older than Granny had been.

"See? She did keep a treasure chest." His voice was full of awe and respect, but then he flashed her a very Rowdy, toothy, I-told-you-so grin. "What do you know, big guy?" he said, addressing Toby. "You found our treasure for us."

Neither of them spoke as she gently pulled off the lid to the box, careful not to mess up any of the decorations.

The very first thing she saw was an envelope—with her and Rowdy's names on it, on top of a layer of tissue paper.

He chuckled. "I thought Jo said we had already seen the last of the envelopes."

"Maybe she didn't know about this one," Angelica suggested in a hushed tone.

"I opened the last one," Rowdy said. "Why don't you do the honors on this one? I suspect it's going to be special."

Angelica did, too. She held her breath as she slid her finger under the seal and pulled out the tri-folded paper.

"It's more than three words," she said. "In fact, it's an honest-to-goodness page-long letter. A story, I think."

Rowdy rested his palms on his thighs and leaned forward. "Something tells me this is going to wrap everything up. As crazy as the last few weeks have been, we could use a little closure. I can't wait to hear it."

A little closure.

Was that what this was? Because even though she'd intended to stop by the hospital and offer Rowdy a proper goodbye, closure, it would not be.

Dear Angelica and Rowdy,

I hope you've had fun taking part in my little scavenger hunt. I know there must have been some confusing moments and many emotional ones, but I'm hoping there were happy ones, too.

"You can say that again," Rowdy muttered.

Angelica lifted an eyebrow. "Are you done?"

"Sorry. Sorry. No more commentating." He grinned and zipped his lips.

I have a little story to tell you, one about Josiah—your Gramps, Angelica—and me. I don't think I ever told you, but Josiah grew up on a cattle ranch. It was my parents who owned the sheep. Anyway, a little after we got engaged— at age seventeen, just like the two of you did— Josiah was helping a neighbor at a roundup and got caught up trying to herd a couple of stray cattle across a stream.

The cows balked, and then his horse bucked and he fell off and busted his leg pretty bad.

Rowdy groaned. "This is starting to feel a little bit too familiar."

"Will you hush and let me keep reading?" she teased.

We didn't have access to the kind of doctors and medicines y'all have today. No physical therapy like that which helped Rowdy recover. Serendipity was too far out and far too small for us to have that kind of help. Some old quack just set the bone and Josiah let it heal on its own.

So as a result, Josiah couldn't ride anymore and because of that he judged himself to be less of a man. I didn't see it, because I was head over ears in love with the stubborn man.

Can you believe he tried to run me off, telling me I ought to marry someone whole—whatever that means? Lord knows all of us are broken. Anyway, raising sheep on a small ranch doesn't necessarily require riding on horseback, and before long there were other mechanical means of transportation.

I thought about leaving town. I almost did. That's why my heart broke when you left without coming to talk to me first, Angelica. I knew just how you felt, and I could have shared this story with you and saved you and Rowdy both a lot of pain.

But you did come back, didn't you? And if you're reading this, then you've been spending time with Rowdy. It took Josiah and me a while to work out our problems, but in the end we said our *I do*'s and we had a good life together. A great one, actually.

God is good, all the time. I hope the treasure you find in this box will mean something special to you. You are both too stubborn for your own good, just like your Gramps and me. I hope you see why I felt I had to nudge you on a little bit with those tasks I gave you. And I hope you know I've done this in love.

Angelica, I really wish I could have met your son, but you know I already love him with my whole heart.

Enjoy the treasure I've left you, and bask in the gift of each other and your son. Gramps and I are looking down on you three and smiling.

Love,

Granny

Angelica pressed her lips together, not even trying to stem the flood of tears pouring down her cheeks.

She'd made so many mistakes, and yet—

Granny was so certain she could rise above them. She had known the mistakes Angelica had made eight years ago, hers and Rowdy's personalities together and apart, and she'd still believed in both of them.

"I think there's something inside this tissue." Rowdy leaned down and picked up a tissue-wrapped package. "Do you want to open it?"

Unable to speak, she shook her head and gestured for him to do it.

Fold by fold, he unwrapped the gift Granny had gone to such lengths to give them.

Rowdy laughed as he undid the last fold.

"Look here. Blue baby booties. Hand knit by Granny Frances, if I don't miss my guess."

"Oh," Angelica exclaimed, clapping a hand over her mouth as a sob escaped. "She made these for Toby."

"Yep," Rowdy agreed. "Wait, though. There's someth—" He cut off his word midsentence. "Well, what do you know?"

"What?"

"I may be thick, but even I can take a hint as bold as this one."

He held up the baby booties. Tied to each one was a ring.

Wedding rings, Angelica realized. Rings that had once belonged to Granny and Gramps.

It took Rowdy a moment to untie Granny's ring from the bootie, but he wasted no time in taking Angelica by the hand and pulling her to her feet.

"We've been through so much," he said, his voice clogging with emotion. "But there is so much more ahead of us. I love you, Angelica, and I always have. I think Granny Frances would like it very much if I put this ring on your finger. And I know I would. I want you to be my wife, and I would be honored to call Toby my son. Will you marry me?"

Only an hour earlier, she'd thought she was leaving Serendipity forever. And now thanks to Granny she would never have to leave it or Rowdy at all. Her heart was so full it was all she could do to nod and allow him to slip Granny's ring on her finger.

"Are you sure you're not just proposing to me for my land?" she teased, her voice cracking with emotion.

He grinned and shrugged. "A man can light two candles with one flame, can't he?"

"Point taken." She paused and tilted her head, her lips matching his contagious smile. "But only if you promise me that at our wedding, we'll be lighting one candle with two flames."

"And maybe a third one for Toby?"

She nodded, her eyes once again filling with happy tears.

"Three candles, one flame," he whispered as his lips hovered over hers. "That sounds just about perfect to me."

* * * * *

Don't miss the latest heartwarming stories about surprise babies leading to lasting love in the COWBOY COUNTRY *miniseries:*

*THE COWBOY'S SURPRISE BABY
THE COWBOY'S TWINS
MISTLETOE DADDY
THE COWBOY'S BABY BLESSING*

*Find these and other great reads at
www.LoveInspired.com.*

Dear Reader,

What fun it is to head back into Serendipity, Texas, and auction off yet another bachelor for the town's First Annual Bachelors and Baskets Auction benefiting the senior center.

I took a bit of a detour with this book. Serendipity is a cattle town and, generally, cattle ranchers and sheep farmers don't mix. But after I read an article about raising sheep, complete with adorable pictures of newborn lambs, I decided Rowdy's and Angelica's families would be exceptions to that rule.

They say art often imitates life. In this case, Angelica's bird phobia? Yeah, that would be me. Dive-bombing hummingbirds rank right up there as one of my worst nightmares.

I'm always delighted to hear from you, dear readers, and I love to connect socially. You can find my website at www.debkastnerbooks.com, where I hope you'll join my mailing list to learn of new projects and special offers. Come join me on Facebook at www.Facebook.com/debkastnerbooks, and you can catch me on Twitter @DebKastner.

Please know that I pray for each and every one of you daily.

Love courageously,

Deb Kastner

COMING NEXT MONTH FROM
Love Inspired®

Available June 19, 2018

HIS NEW AMISH FAMILY
The Amish Bachelors • by Patricia Davids

Desperate to stop her *Englisch* cousin from selling the farm her uncle promised to her, widow Clara Fisher seeks the help of auctioneer Paul Bowman. Paul's always been a wandering spirit, but will sweet, stubborn Clara and her children suddenly fill his empty life with family and love?

HER FORGIVING AMISH HEART
Women of Lancaster County • by Rebecca Kertz

Leah Stoltzfus hasn't forgiven Henry Yoder for betraying her family years earlier. But Henry is a changed man. And when a family secret is unearthed, shaking Leah to her core, he's determined to support her. If only she could leave the past behind and open her heart to him...

THE SOLDIER'S REDEMPTION
Redemption Ranch • by Lee Tobin McClain

Finn Gallagher's drawn to his new rescue-dog caretaker, Kayla White, and her little boy. But the single mother's running from something in her past. And as he begins wishing the little family could be *his*, Finn must convince her to trust him with her secret.

FALLING FOR THE COWGIRL
Big Heart Ranch • by Tina Radcliffe

Hiring Amanda "AJ" McAlester as his assistant at the Big Heart Ranch isn't foreman Travis Maxwell's first choice—but his sisters insist she's perfect for the job. But with money on the line, AJ and her innovative ideas could put him at risk of losing everything...including his heart.

HIS TWO LITTLE BLESSINGS
Liberty Creek • by Mia Ross

When the school board threatens to cut her art program, Emma Calhoun plans to fight for the job she loves. And with banker Rick Marshall on board to help, she might just succeed. But will the handsome widower and his sweet little girls burrow their way into her heart?

THE COWBOY'S LITTLE GIRL
Bent Creek Blessings • by Kat Brookes

Cowboy Tucker Wade discovers he has a daughter he never knew about when his late wife's twin sister shows up on his doorstep. Now it's up to Autumn Myers to decide if he can be the kind of daddy her niece deserves.

LOOK FOR THESE AND OTHER LOVE INSPIRED BOOKS WHEREVER BOOKS ARE SOLD, INCLUDING MOST BOOKSTORES, SUPERMARKETS, DISCOUNT STORES AND DRUGSTORES.

LICNM0618

SPECIAL EXCERPT FROM

Love Inspired®

Her family's future in the balance, can Clara Fisher find a way to save her home?

Read on for a sneak preview of
HIS NEW AMISH FAMILY *by* Patricia Davids,
the next book in **THE AMISH BACHELORS** *miniseries,*
available in July 2018 from Love Inspired.

Paul Bowman leaned forward in his seat to get a good look at the farm as they drove up. Both the barn and the house were painted white and appeared in good condition. He made a quick mental appraisal of the equipment he saw, then jotted down numbers in a small notebook he kept in his pocket.

"What is she doing here?" The anger in his client Ralph's voice shocked Paul.

He followed Ralph's line of sight and spied an Amish woman sitting on a suitcase on the front porch of the house. She wore a simple pale blue dress with an apron of matching material and a black cape thrown back over her shoulders. Her wide-brimmed black traveling bonnet hid her hair. She looked hot, dusty and tired. She held a girl of about three or four on her lap. The child clung tightly to her mother. A boy a few years older leaned against the door behind her holding a large calico cat.

"Who is she?" Paul asked.

"That is my annoying cousin, Clara Fisher." Ralph opened his car door and got out. Paul did the same.

The woman glared at both men. "Why are there padlocks on the doors, Ralph? Eli never locked his home."

"They are there to keep unwanted visitors out. What are you doing here?" Ralph demanded.

"I live here. May I have the keys, please? My children and I are weary."

Ralph's eyebrows snapped together in a fierce frown. "What do you mean you live here?"

"What part did you fail to understand, Ralph? I… live…here," she said slowly.

Ralph's face darkened with anger. Paul had to turn away to keep from laughing.

She might look small, but she was clearly a woman to be reckoned with. She reminded him of an angry mama cat all fluffed up and spitting-mad. He rubbed a hand across his mouth to hide a grin. His movement caught her attention, and she pinned her deep blue gaze on him. "Who are you?"

He stopped smiling. "My name is Paul Bowman. I'm an auctioneer. Mr. Hobson has hired me to get this property ready for sale."

Don't miss
HIS NEW AMISH FAMILY by Patricia Davids,
available July 2018 wherever
Love Inspired® books and ebooks are sold.

www.LoveInspired.com

Looking for inspiration in tales
of hope, faith and heartfelt romance?

Check out **Love Inspired**® and
Love Inspired® **Suspense** books!

New books available every month!

LIGENRE2018